YORK NC

General Editors: Prc
of Stirling) & Profes:
University of Beirut)

Daniel Defoe

ROBINSON CRUSOE

Notes by A.R. Humphreys
MA (CAMBRIDGE) AM (HARVARD)
Professor Emeritus, University of Leicester

YORK PRESS
Immeuble Esseily, Place Riad Solh, Beirut.

LONGMAN GROUP UK LIMITED
Longman House, Burnt Mill, Harlow,
Essex CM20 2JE, England
Associated companies, branches and representatives
throughout the world

© Librairie du Liban 1980

All rights reserved; no part of this publication may be reproduced,
stored in a retrieval system, or transmitted in any form or by any
means, electronic, mechanical, photocopying, recording, or otherwise
without either the prior written permission of the Publishers or a
licence permitting restricted copying in the United Kingdom issued by
the Copyright Licensing Agency Ltd, 90 Tottenham Court Road, London, W1P 9HE.

First published 1980
Seventh impression 1993

ISBN 0-582-78111-6

Produced by Longman Singapore Publishers Pte Ltd
Printed in Singapore

Contents

Part 1: Introduction *page* 5
   Robinson Crusoe's status   5
   Defoe's life and time   6
   Preliminaries   11
   A note on the text   15

Part 2: Summaries   16
   A general study   16
   Detailed summaries   17

Part 3: Commentary   42
   What sort of novel?   42
   Form and themes   47
   Characterisation: Crusoe himself   48
   Characterisation: other characters   52
   Style and expression   53
   An age of enterprise   60
   Religious bearings   65

Part 4: Hints for study   67
   Key points for attention   67
   Significant passages   68
   Arranging material for answers   68
   Specimen questions   70
   Model answers   70

Part 5: Suggestions for further reading   78

   The author of these notes   80

Part 1
Introduction

Robinson Crusoe's status

An excellent short study of Defoe, by James Sutherland, in the British Council's 'Writers and their Work' series, starts with a telling point, that we feel surprised to find *Robinson Crusoe* a literary classic. Classics are usually less entertaining. It certainly is a classic, however, if to be avidly read by an extraordinary variety of readers in many lands for the past two and a half centuries (and likely to continue so for the next two and a half) earns classic status—status, that is, which the dictionary defines as 'of the highest class or rank, ... having literary or historical associations; traditionally accepted, long-established', and, we might add, with powerful representative meaning.

Samuel Taylor Coleridge (1772–1834), the great Romantic poet and critic, annotated his copy of *Robinson Crusoe* with the reflection that:

> The writer who makes me sympathise with his presentations with the *whole* of my being is more estimable than the writer who calls forth and appeals to but a part ...; and again, he who makes me forget my *specific* class, character, and circumstances, raises me into the universal man. Now this is Defoe's excellence. You become a man while you read.

Robinson Crusoe's first critic, however, thought otherwise. He was Charles Gildon, a minor literary contemporary of Defoe's, and he poked fun at its religious moralisings, among other things. To him it was far from a book for 'the *whole*' being. He fancied Defoe boasting to Crusoe that he, Crusoe, was the idol of the simple-minded:

> There is not an old woman that can go the price of it but buys thy *Life and Adventures*, and leaves it as a legacy, with the *Pilgrim's Progress*, the *Practice of Piety*, and *God's Revenge against Murder*, to her posterity.

From a far higher standpoint the Victorian scholar and critic, Leslie Stephen, judged it 'a book for boys rather than men, [since it] falls short of any high intellectual standard'. Only the naive, evidently, could be engrossed by it.

Yet Alexander Pope, the eighteenth century's greatest poet, and

Samuel Johnson, its greatest critic, praised it. 'Was there', Johnson asked, 'ever yet anything written by mere man that was wished longer by its readers, excepting *Don Quixote, Robinson Crusoe,* and the *Pilgrim's Progress?*' (No doubt he meant the original *Robinson Crusoe*: Defoe's two continuations* are by no means too short.) Jean-Jacques Rousseau, most thought-provoking of eighteenth-century philosophers, thought it the best reading an ideal education could offer for inspiring a child's mind, and for Karl Marx it was a classic of the labour theory of value. Various major significances have been attributed to it—the sturdy independence of religious energies, the thrust of the merchant class, the enterprise of Western economic life, the universal thirst for adventure, the satisfactions of work, the edification of spiritual awakening, and so on. As for its technique, Defoe has been judged a writer whose naturalness lacks art, or (by the French critic Henri Taine) one whose 'lack of art becomes a profound art', or (by the English novelist Virginia Woolf) actually 'a great artist'. 'There are many ways of approaching this classical volume', Virginia Woolf remarks, 'but which shall we choose?' Her own way is to feel it stretching the imagination widely, from practical satisfactions ('a plain earthenware pot') to spiritual resonances ('remote islands and the solitudes of the human soul'): that is its spread.

There is, then, as you will see from the views outlined above a wide range of critical attitudes to *Robinson Crusoe*.

Defoe's life and time

Born in 1660, Daniel Foe (he added the De about 1695 to suggest higher status) was the son of a London citizen who supported a religious sect outside the official Church of England. Such men, called 'Dissenters', suffered certain penalties; they were, for instance, debarred from the universities of Oxford and Cambridge and so from qualifying (except in Scotland) for the learned professions. Daniel remained a Dissenter throughout his life but was broadminded about other persuasions: this tolerance resulted from his own common sense, his experience of men, and his age's trend towards moderation—he was generally forward-looking in religious and social views. His religious individualism convinced him, as *Robinson Crusoe* holds, that God communicates not through church formalities but directly with each soul. This conviction makes all men equal in God's eyes and all are responsible for that self-scrutiny within, and that sign-seeking without, which show whether the soul pleases its maker.

This means the opposite of hermit-like withdrawal, of what Milton

*See *A note on the text* p. 15

rejected as 'fugitive and cloistered virtue, unexercised and unbreathed'. It means vigorous work in one's God-appointed business in life. Not only Dissenters believed this; the whole age was busy with national expansion (see below, page 60). But Dissenters, excluded from the traditional professions, were specially concerned to show that God approved them in other walks of life, and they strove strongly for business success.

Defoe was educated at a Dissenting academy, where the modernist curriculum included history, modern languages, and the sciences, as well as divinity and moral philosophy. (A fellow-pupil was one Timothy Cruso, whose name Defoe somehow recalled nearly fifty years afterwards.) He aimed at becoming a Dissenting preacher but later wrote that it was his 'disaster first to be set aside for, and then to be set apart from, . . . that sacred ministry' (*Review*, 22 October 1709). The reasons for this setting apart are unknown: perhaps he needed a wider sphere. Yet though life called him to worldly courses he remained active in matters of faith, both inwardly (concerning the individual's spiritual state) and outwardly (concerning the ethics of belief and the conditions of religious observance).

He put himself to trade, and was described as 'merchant' when he married in 1684. His enterprises required long journeys in Britain and on the Continent; like his fictional heroes he knew the world. His fortunes varied; like Crusoe he was not only ambitious but overadventurous; he went bankrupt in 1692 but strove with fair success to repay creditors from the profits of a tile factory he ran. Simultaneously he began political work, which he kept up through his life for one or other political party. Roughly speaking, the Tories (forerunners of the modern Conservatives) were for maintaining royal power, strengthening the established Church of England, and supporting the traditional country landowners against the moneyed men of commerce, while the Whigs (forerunners of the modern Liberals) were for restricting royal power, extending religious freedom, and encouraging commercial progress. Both parties had extreme wings (which on either side Defoe opposed) and moderate centres (for either of which Defoe worked, as he judged the national needs warranted).

By 1700 he had a broad and detailed grasp of commercial and political life. He was also writing fast—the scope and number of his publications are almost incredible. His *Essay upon Projects* (1698) is a vigorous programme for economic and social advance; the same topics still engrossed him thirty years later, in *The Complete English Tradesman* (1725) and *A Plan of the English Commerce* (1728). In between, along with numerous other works, he produced two extended surveys of the nation's affairs: these were a periodical, the *Review* (1704–13, originally centred on the English-French war then raging, later extended to affairs of many kinds), and *A Tour thro' the Whole Island of Great Britain* (1724–26, an encyclopedic account of topography, occupations, and conditions). The *Review*, written single-handed, at first weekly, later twice or thrice weekly, is by far the biggest journalistic achievement of any English writer, and the *Tour* is an invaluable record of local life. Both are lively commentaries on practical affairs, viewed with strikingly enlightened eyes.

Political and religious interests rivalled economic ones. In 1701 he supported King William III with *The Trueborn Englishman*, for William, a Dutchman who gained the crown in 1688 because his wife was the deposed James II's sister, provoked hostility through favours shown to his Dutch followers and was lampooned in *The Foreigners* (1700) by a literary satirist, John Tutchin. Defoe's reply was a pungent poem deriding descendants of 'That het'rogeneous thing, an *Englishman*', who complained about William's foreign origin. The English, Defoe reminded them, are an 'amphibious ill-born mob', the 'barb'rous offspring' of invaders: who are they to claim purity? The poem is rollicking polemic in the idiom of popular gusto and by its hard-hitting and substantial contents has far more than temporary effect.

The year 1702 saw another daring venture, a brilliant pamphlet, *The Shortest Way with the Dissenters*. This parodied a bigoted churchman urging savage punishments for Dissenters, and religious tempers ran so high that, though its extravagance might have given it away as ironical, churchmen hailed it with delight (which their discovery of the truth turned to fury) and Dissenters with horror (which their later relief did not turn to joy). Defoe was sentenced to be pilloried, exposed to the mob. He refused to hide away; instead he published his powerful *Hymn to the Pillory*, a work whose exuberance illustrates James Sutherland's comment on his poetic qualities, that he was 'carried along willingly and at times recklessly by the excitement of composition'. His reward came when, instead of being tormented, he was hero-worshipped by the crowd, among whom the *Hymn* was selling rapidly.

Yet the affair bankrupted his business, and thereafter he depended for money on political services and writing. He travelled the country as a political agent and, under various aliases, reported provincial feelings to London; in an important phase of negotiation he sounded Scottish reactions to the proposed union with England which came about in 1707. Later, for the Whigs, he worked his way into the management of Tory journals so as to moderate their tone; this questionable tactic made sense when tensions ran dangerously high. Defoe could claim that all his efforts, for whichever side, aimed at constructive moderation, and on this ground he based a manifesto to Parliament in 1701, *Legion's Memorial*, and his *Appeal to Honour and Justice* in 1715. The former, citing traditional English justice, summoned Parliament to free certain petitioners who had been imprisoned for urging defence measures against France, and in this bold aim it succeeded. The latter pleaded that his propagandist exertions were inspired by the nation's genuine interests.

What, though, has this to do with his literary work? Its relevance is that it often called for impersonation, for presenting another's point of view, and for a style readily and popularly acceptable. At this Defoe was adept; he could convincingly assume various identities, though by doing so in *The Shortest Way* he had landed himself in trouble. During the Scottish negotiations he wrote a letter (26 November 1706) describing the guises and opinions he adopted: 'I am perfectly unsuspected as corresponding with anyone in England. I converse with Presbyterian, Episcopal, Dissenter, Papist, and Non-Juror ... I talk to everybody in their own way.' In life, as in fiction, he could submerge himself in role-playing; this needed alertness, adaptability, and a wide command of idioms, ideas, and skills. The letter relates also his dealings not only with religious adherents but with shipbuilders, traders, merchants, lawyers, and manufacturers, all on their own terms, and to this range he could add journalistic and political adroitness too.

Such masquerading meant also that fact and fiction were interchangeable; the real authentic and the bogus authentic were virtually indistinguishable. By hallucinatory sleight-of-hand Defoe could always create a fictional reality as convincing as the real thing.

Often, indeed, readers have felt uncertain whether he was writing fact or fiction. *A True Relation of the Apparition of Mrs Veal* (1706) is a case in point. It claims to be absolutely authentic—'This relation is matter of fact, and attended with such circumstances as may induce any reasonable man to believe it'. Yet it was long taken for fiction, though now it is known to be retelling a ghost story then believed to be true, a story of which there are accounts earlier than Defoe's. He is not really masquerading here, though he purports to tell the story through a Justice of the Peace ('a very intelligent person'), for the narrator's personality does not affect the story save insofar as it guarantees its truthfulness. Yet Defoe shows masterly skill in hypnotising the reader by ingenious detail, subtle shading, and narrative clarity. Is this fact, or fiction? It partakes of both: it uses the supposed facts of the case, and it authenticates these with an art born of Defoe's vivid conception. The apparent lack of authorial creation is very creative indeed.

Dissenters often disliked fiction, arguing that honest fact is the only proper thing. In the 'Apology' which Bunyan prefixed to *The Pilgrim's Progress* (1678) he recognised their scruples, and he defended his fiction by claiming to follow biblical examples, to seek 'the advance of truth', and to gain a hearing for his message, provided that no deceit was practised on 'words, things, readers'. Defoe was less scrupulous than Bunyan; what urged him on was an immense zest for recording the world's activities, and in this urge religious principles played only a subordinate though significant part. Yet as he evolved from the actual authenticity of *Mrs Veal* or *The Storm* (1704—an account of a tremendous tempest of 1703), through the plausible motions of *The Shortest Way* or of ironical pamphlets 'recommending' political causes he really opposed, to lively fictions like *The Family Instructor* (1715—domestic dialogues with moral lessons), he could always claim that his purpose was the cause of moral truth. *Robinson Crusoe*, he straightfacedly maintains in its Preface, is 'a just history of fact'; it also serves 'to justify and honour the wisdom of Providence'. Modern readers may be less impressed by this than were Gildon's old women, yet the book's religious elements have recently been better valued than they used to be. Defoe's fictional 'truth' includes much psychology of religious experience; as James Sutherland observes, 'he never lost the earnestness, and the stubborn conviction of having an "inner light", that are at once the source of the Puritan's strength and of his limitation'.

The Life and Strange Surprizing Adventures of Robinson Crusoe (April 1719) was Defoe's first novel; he was fifty-eight. This late creative outburst is astonishing, but scarcely more so than what followed. The book immediately succeeded, and *Farther Adventures* (August 1719) and *Serious Reflections . . . of Robinson Crusoe* (1720) rapidly followed. Other substantial works appeared in 1720, including *Memoirs of a Cavalier* (allegedly authentic papers of a seventeenth-century gentleman-at-arms) and *The Life, Adventures, and Piracies of the Famous Captain Singleton* (fictitious hazards at sea and on a trans-African journey). 1722 saw several minor and three major works—*The Fortunes and Misfortunes of the Famous Moll Flanders* (an 'autobiography' almost as impressive as Crusoe's), *A Journal of the Plague Year* (vivid reconstruction of London's great plague of 1665), and *The History and Remarkable Life of the truly Honourable Colonel Jacque* (the beginning of which is the movingly imagined story of a London waif). In 1724 appeared *The Fortunate Mistress . . . Roxana* (a highlife parallel to low-life *Moll Flanders*) and the first part of the *Tour thro' the Whole Island of Great Britain*, the rest following in 1725 and 1726. This completed Defoe's major work, and the appearance during his seventh decade of twelve substantial volumes marks the climax of an astoundingly enterprising life. He died in 1731.

Preliminaries

Three preliminaries to *Robinson Crusoe* offer themselves—the impact of travel narratives, the vogue of spiritual autobiography, and the emergence of the novel. Other contextual matters will be discussed below; see pages 60 to 66.

(i) Travel Narratives

Robinson Crusoe contains foreign experience, exotic scenes, and survival skills characteristic of travellers' journals, some of which markedly influenced it. It owes its main basis to the story of a Scottish seaman, Alexander Selkirk (1676–1721), related in *A Cruising Voyage Round the World* (1712) by a Captain Woodes Rogers, which had a second edition in 1718, the year before *Robinson Crusoe*. Sailing in February 1709 by Juan Fernandez island, off the west of South America, Captain Rogers discovered Selkirk, stranded there in 1704 for quarrelling with his captain. Like Crusoe, after initial melancholy, Selkirk 'conquer[ed] all the Inconveniences of his Solitude', but unlike Crusoe he almost forgot how to speak. Though less well equipped than Crusoe, he built huts thatched with grass and lined with goat-skins: he cultivated turnips derived from those planted by earlier visitors: he carved on trees his name and various dates, sewed goat-skin clothes with a needle made from a nail, tamed kids, 'and to divert himself would now and then sing and dance with them and his cats'. His spare life so toughened him that he could outrun wild goats and Rogers's bulldog. Not least notably, he consoled himself with psalm-singing and religious reflection so that (like Crusoe) 'he was a better Christian while in this solitude than ever he was before'. He reached London in October 1711.

Selkirk's story became popular. The journalist Richard Steele retold it in 1713 in his paper, *The Englishman*, having several times met him in London. (Whether Defoe ever did so is not known.) But other precedents for Crusoe were also available: Rogers himself mentions a sailor described in Captain Basil Ringrose's *History of the Buccaneers* (1685), who was shipwrecked on Juan Fernandez and marooned for five years there, and a South American Indian who, hunting ashore from an English ship, was abandoned when a storm blew up and had to survive alone for three years.

The greatest seafaring narrative, however, is Captain William Dampier's *A New Voyage Round the World* (1697). Dampier was an eminent navigator and, in fact, Rogers's pilot when he rescued Selkirk. He wrote capably with much human interest about his crews and native life, in the style, he declared himself, of the practical seaman who wants to be clear and cares little for polish. The reason why Defoe put Crusoe's island not in the Pacific but in the Atlantic just east of Trinidad may be to avoid too close a parallel with Selkirk, but it may reflect his interest in Sir Walter Raleigh's *Discovery of the Empire of Guiana* (1596: Defoe published a version in 1720) and also the appearance at that location, in a map in Dampier's volume, of a cluster of islands (which do not in fact exist). Many of Defoe's Brazilian details resemble Dampier's. Dampier describes islands off South America abounding (like Crusoe's) with goats and tortoises, one having (like Crusoe's again) an eastward reef fatal to shipping. He tells how 'pereagoes or canoes' are (like Crusoe's) fashioned from hollowed cedar trunks, and how natives split trees to make planks, and form wooden dwellings against cliff faces, entering them with ladders. Many such details are not unique to Dampier, but so much in his account foreshadows *Robinson Crusoe* that influences from so notable a work seem likely.

Defoe may have sought further. Captain Robert Knox's *Nineteen Years in Captivity in . . . Ceylon* (1681) has been cited as a possible source, particularly for Crusoe's long journey across Asia in *Farther Adventures*, for Knox escaped, with companions, by a hazardous cross-country trek. His stress on religious succour is noteworthy: buying a Bible from a Cingalese native he opened it at random (like Crusoe), found consoling texts, and believed his deliverance miraculous because 'the hand of God did eminently appear' in leading him through the wilderness. Whether or not Defoe read him, Knox's trust in God parallels the growing earnestness of Crusoe's redemption.

(ii) Spiritual Autobiography

This aspect of Knox leads appropriately to *Robinson Crusoe*'s religious context; the best guide to this is G.A. Starr's *Defoe and Spiritual Autobiography* (1965). The seventeenth century, with its religious ardours, had multiplied confessions of God's dealings with sinners, dealings which prompted anguished self-scrutinies and diary records of spiritual awakenings and the raptures of the redeemed soul. The humblest events could seem significant—supernatural manifestations were not needed, though they might present themselves in visions. Sinners might record their good or ill use of God-given time, and compile balance-sheets of spiritual pros and cons like Crusoe's. The biblical parable of the Prodigal Son, the wanderer who leaves his loving parents for a wicked life and returns ruined at last to a loving welcome, was repeatedly echoed; Crusoe himself mentions it when, venturing from home, he is storm-struck at sea and wrecked at Yarmouth. The soul might for a while be deaf to God's promptings, vainly striving to go its own way, only to be tossed by spiritual tempests until it acknowledged its fault. Once converted, it would feel bound to proclaim salvation to others.

This clearly resembled Crusoe's experience. True, his book moderates the intense emotion often proclaimed in seventeenth-century spiritual autobiography (most famously, for instance, in Bunyan's significantly named *Grace Abounding to the Chief of Sinners* (1666)). Defoe's age was not one for extremes, and both his temperament and technique forbade extravagance. Yet we need not assume that to his contemporaries Crusoe's religious experiences were as sober as they may seem to us; sympathetically read, they reveal surprising feeling. Strong religious feeling was commoner in Defoe's day than in ours (though religious revivalism can still be ecstatic), and if he conveyed it temperately he, and his readers, doubtless responded warmly. His book is mainly a book of this world, yet resonances from another world sound powerfully within it. (Further comment on the book's religious bearings follows below: see pages 65 and 66.)

(iii) The Emergence of the Novel

To define a 'novel' exactly is impossible, but a fair lead is offered by Dr Johnson in *The Rambler* (No. 4, 31 March 1750), when he comments that his contemporaries read with particular pleasure books which 'exhibit life in its true state, diversified only by accidents that daily happen in the world, and influenced by passions and qualities which are really to be found in conversing with mankind.' Typically the novel is 'life in its true state', credible successions of events and the recognisable passions of mankind.

Its needs include convincing time sequence, convincing place and time setting, and convincing character reacting to convincing circumstances. These needs were more evident by the late seventeenth century than they had been earlier (though of course stories have existed from time immemorial); contributory influences were the growth of scientific and economic realism, and the psychological analysis of personality which Locke conducted in his *Essay concerning Human Understanding* (1690), a work fundamental for eighteenth-century thought. Few narratives before Defoe's suggest his kind of reality, of realistic persons in realistic circumstances performing likely actions in likely time sequence.

Medieval romances appeal by remoteness of events, characters, and atmosphere. So too, through romantic ideality, do Elizabethan 'novels' like Sidney's *Arcadia* (1590) or Greene's *Pandosto* (1588) or Lodge's *Rosalynde* (1590), all sources for Shakespeare, or poetic fantasies like Spenser's *The Faerie Queene* (1590–6). There are picturesque Elizabethan short stories of gross or grotesque low life, unpretentious homely fictions like Deloney's *Thomas of Reading* (1612) or *John Winchcombe* (1619), and extravagant travel-caprices like Nashe's picaresque *The Unfortunate Traveller* (1594). But nowhere is life realistically rendered at length.

A few late seventeenth-century works approach the novel more closely. Besides potboiling social anecdotes and rogue biographies which anticipated at a low level the appeal of *Moll Flanders, Roxana*, and *Colonel Jacque*, there appeared Henry Neville's brief *Isle of Pines* (1668), Bunyan's *The Pilgrim's Progress* (1678), Aphra Behn's *Oroonoko; or, The Royal Slave* (1688), and Congreve's *Incognita* (1691). *The Isle of Pines* tells of shipwreck in the Indian Ocean, with much of Defoe's factual zest. But the narrator, George Pine, lives in such fertile promiscuity with several women castaways that by the time he is eighty he has 1789 descendants (isle of Pines indeed!), and the story (too slight really to count as a novel) combines exotic realism with erotic fantasy. *The Pilgrim's Progress* is a masterpiece but also differs from the true novel, since its graphic surface is mainly a guise for allegorical meanings. *Oroonoko* is a powerful story of a princely African negro, enslaved and tortured to death by white colonists: it is splendidly told but leans rather to the heroic romance than the regular novel. *Incognita* is light social comedy. None of these stories convincingly heralds that substantial lifelikeness which is the novel's special world, though the popularity in one way of *Don Quixote* and in another way of the periodical essay portraying character and society showed a growing taste for intelligent fiction.

Practised in realistic journalism, in skilful masquerading, in vivid accounts of projects and trade and travel expressed in forthright prose, Defoe moved almost automatically to achieve the first prose-fictional story of a fully credible, fully extended human being grappling with lifelike circumstances. By so doing he created, with no sign of deliberate intent, the dominant literary form for the following centuries, in a masterpiece achieved, it would seem, spontaneously and unselfconsciously. *Robinson Crusoe* is a landmark.

By comparing *Robinson Crusoe* with the above brief outlines of earlier fiction, you can consider why it marks a great advance on previous works.

A note on the text

The first edition in 1719 was followed, and continues to be followed, by numerous others, and by translations, adaptations, and imitations in many languages. There are many sound modern editions: among the most serviceable is that by Angus Ross in the Penguin English Library, published by Penguin Books Ltd, Harmondsworth, Middlesex, England, Penguin Books Inc., 3300 Clipper Mill Road, Baltimore 11, Maryland, USA, and Penguin Books Ltd, Ringwood, Victoria, Australia. As well as notes and a glossary it contains a good introduction, and it reprints Captain Woodes Rogers's and Richard Steele's accounts of the rescue of Alexander Selkirk, from *A Cruising Voyage Round the World* and *The Englishman* respectively. Page references below are those of this edition, but identifying tags are given for readers with other texts. *Robinson Crusoe* refers in this study to the first of Defoe's three narratives, the others being referred to as *Farther Adventures* and *Serious Reflections*.

Part 2

Summaries
of ROBINSON CRUSOE

A general summary

Robinson Crusoe, son of a German merchant settled in England, is urged by his father to follow a career in trade, this being the reliable road to modest prosperity. A strange impulse, however, impels him to rebel and to seek adventures; this rebellion he later considers to be a sin, visited by divine punishment in the form of his misfortunes. His first sea-voyage ends in shipwreck, but he tries again, prospering at first but soon falling captive to a Turkish raider off the Moroccan coast. Rescued by a Portuguese ship he is taken to Brazil, where he succeeds as a planter. But again an urge to travel overcomes him, and again he suffers shipwreck. He is cast, alone, on the shore of an uninhabited island off the mouth of the Orinoco River in South America. He describes the measures he takes for his immediate survival, and then his growing command of his situation. He proves admirably resourceful in making tools, clothes, equipment, and shelter, but he also begins to reflect on his life and conduct, and this leads him gradually to religious faith and gratitude.

After years of loneliness he is one day terrified to come on the remains of a cannibal feast. During a later cannibal raid he rescues an intended victim and trains him as his servant and friend, naming him Friday after the day of his rescue. Together they save a Spanish captain and also Friday's father from a further cannibal feast, and learn that the Spaniard's crew have escaped to the mainland, whither the Spanish captain and Friday's father are sent to bring them to the island. Before they return, however, Crusoe and Friday rescue an English captain and two other victims from the mutinous crew of an English ship; the mutineers are overcome, the captain restored, and the ship lands Crusoe in England after thirty-five years' absence, together with the faithful Friday.

The final pages relate how he visits Lisbon, finds that his Brazilian estate has flourished and that he is prosperous, and reaches England again with Friday after a hazardous crossing of the Pyrenees. He marries, but his wife dies and his roving disposition asserts itself again. He revisits his island, now populated by the Spanish and English sailors left there, and as the book ends Crusoe half-promises a further instalment of the island story and further adventures.

Detailed summaries

Though *Robinson Crusoe* is not presented in chapters as are most later novels (their authors sensing that so free a form benefits from clear staging), it may be usefully phased in the divisions suggested below. There is nothing authoritative about these but they conveniently clarify the attention. They do, too, reflect Defoe's skill at short-length episodes, and so follow the means by which the narrative grew. As already mentioned in 'A note on the text', page references are those of the Penguin English Library edition, but identifying tags are given for readers with other texts.

Preface

Though brief, this makes significant points: first, that the story, because surprising and varied, is calculated to be popular—a surmise marvellously vindicated by the wildfire-like spread of its appeal; second, that it is authentic, a 'just history of fact' merely transmitted by the editor to the press (Defoe and others habitually practised such stratagems—the best way to recommend fiction was to offer it as fact); third, that it avoids romantic extravagances; and fourth, that its religious tenor points to the righteous conduct of life. Impressively straightfaced, Defoe presents his ingenious fiction as honest, entertaining, and improving fact, and congratulates himself as mere editor on benefiting the public.

Pages 27 to 38: from 'I was born in the year 1632' to 'ashamed of the returning, which only can make them be esteemed wise men'.

This first phase introduces Crusoe's family, relates his adventurous impulse, sees him tested by his first seastorm, and brings him to London. A sequence of options opens the road from obedient orthodoxy to dangerous, exhilarating independence, a process doubtless which Defoe himself knew as he passed from his father's settled business and faith to his own risky career.

He establishes the story by a firm, expository style. Nothing is vague or questionable: these are the convincing facts. Yet at once tensions (discreetly inserted) are sensed within so normal a setting. One elder brother has been killed in Flanders after (as we are to learn a little later) rejecting his father's 'earnest persuasions' to stay at home. A second brother has vanished. Clearly the younger generation have all felt the 'rambling thoughts' that stir Robinson, and a family drama is set up between old and young. Defoe effects this effortlessly, firm facts and psychological pulls interacting. He achieves a moving human situation as Crusoe's father urges the value of the 'middle state' with real warmth of concern and at last with manly sorrow. It is evident that, with disciplined sincerity, Defoe can dramatise true feeling as well as impart true facts.

Playing against paternal conservatism is its antithesis, the irrational dynamic urge which presses men forward, 'something fatal in that propension of nature' which goads Crusoe into recklessness. This might be mere convention, the Prodigal Son's proverbial wilfulness. Yet a sense of mysterious compulsion invests it, surely a further reflection of Defoe's own restlessness driving him from safety and success into unknown hazards. These obsessions form a large part of the book's psychological power: there is no 'prose and reason' about them, but rather a stormy imaginative urgency. Far from personifying hard-headed practicality Crusoe burns with romantic desire, seeks new horizons, deserts the attainable for the unattainable, while always keeping his wits and courage strong, and supporting reverses dauntlessly. Seafaring in Defoe's time meant danger and violence; preferring it to security at home, Crusoe flies in the face of Providence. The expansive aspiration he shows thus early proves him much more than an indomitable handyman.

Conventionally, he laments his wilfulness and attributes it to something beyond his control—'my ill fate pushed me on now with an obstinacy that nothing could resist'. Here, though, emerges a very human ambiguity: he wants reckless experience, yet laments his wanting it. Yielding to the 'fatal' (that is, fateful) impulse he judges himself 'wicked'; yet later, contemplating this irrational instigation, he feels it 'a strange impression' like those 'secret hints or pressings of my mind' which are God's instructions directing him subconsciously to opportune action.

This, though confused logically, is very interesting. If 'fatal' impulses sometimes overcome his reason and prompt him to 'wicked' courses, are they distinguishable from the 'secret hints' which also sometimes overcome his reason but result in good ones? Is he a weathercock blown by every wind? Is his valued reason any use? How is rational foresight related to irrational energy? Can 'wicked' impulses be distinguished from God-given ones only when we know the outcome? Is Crusoe not illogical in condemning the one and revering the other? Yet if illogical he is nonetheless human. Men of strong feelings do recognise irresistible promptings which lead sometimes to ill, sometimes to good; which are which, is hard to determine. Reason strives to judge, and deserves respect; yet reason is a regulating, not a dynamic, force. As Pope puts it in his *Essay on Man* (1733), 'Reason the card [the seaman's guiding compass], but Passion is the gale [the impelling wind]'. Particularly to the creative mind is risk essential:— prosaic success is less what life wants than are the leaps, for ill or good, of primary and mysterious feelings. Less and less does Crusoe, or Defoe, seem the representative practical bourgeois; his mind, a critic has recently said, 'is not only original but almost eccentric'.

As Crusoe ventures into the world the story moves energetically, canvassing conflicting opinions, and powerfully describing the storms interpreted as God's wrath. Why, one may ask, should Heaven afflict so many others also to punish Crusoe? But Crusoe follows the superstitious tradition which takes general disasters to be punishment for particular sinners. The whole narration is alive, in idiom and event, the most vigorously naturalistic writing yet in English fiction.

NOTES AND GLOSSARY
battle near Dunkirk: an English army fought against the Spaniards at Dunkirk, near the French-Dutch border, in 1656
mechanick part of mankind: manual workers
Hull ... Humber: Hull is a port on the River Humber, on the east coast of England
repenting prodigal: in the Bible, a young man leaves home rebelliously but returns years later, ruined, to a loving welcome
least: lest
a cap full of wind: a passing gust
Yarmouth roads: safe anchoring waters, at Yarmouth, an east coast port
rid: floated at anchor
tided it: floated with the tide
ground-tackle: devices for anchoring
strike our top-masts: lower the upper mast sections
rid forecastle in: took water over the ship's forward quarters
our anchor had come home: our anchor no longer held the ground
sheet anchor: largest anchor, for emergencies
vered out to the better end: extended to the very end (generally, the 'bitter end', the end attached to the 'bitt', a post fixed in the deck)
stupid: in a state of stupor
steerage: cheapest passenger area, astern
by the board: overboard
at all adventures: at any risk

sprit-sail: small sail below bowsprit, the pole projecting forward from the bow
more sensible: more aware
the hold: the interior, for stowing cargo
swim: stay afloat
rid it out: survived the storm
halled: hauled
Winterton ... Cromer: towns, like Yarmouth, on the eastern bulge of England
Blessed Saviour's parable: story, told by Jesus, of the Prodigal Son (see earlier note)
Jonah ... Tarshish: in the Bible, God commands the prophet Jonah to denounce a wicked city, but Jonah takes ship to flee to the foreign port of Tarshish. A storm strikes the ship and the sailors fling Jonah overboard
excursion of his spirits: outburst of his feelings

Pages 38 to 54: from 'In this state of life, however' to 'what to do next with myself I was now to consider'.

This phase is the admirably told story of Crusoe's capture by a Turkish rover of Sallee, adventurous escape, and rescue by a Portuguese ship. In his moralising mood the experience qualifies as punishment for his disobeying his father, 'the most unfortunate of all enterprises'. Yet it reads as a most satisfactorily exciting episode: Crusoe is recurrently caught in the dilemma of self-condemnation which deplores his exploits, and inner satisfaction which thrills at audacities. The former has all the propriety, the latter all the life-blood.

It is noteworthy how much decency Crusoe finds in the workaday world. He had already done so with the humane magistrates and brave sailors at Yarmouth, the 'pretty good company' he falls into in London, and the 'honest and plain-dealing' English captain whose rectitude enables him to increase his trading gains. Repeatedly when we might expect to find brutality inserted to give a strong effect to the narrative we find its opposite. Escaping from slavery Crusoe is saved by a wonderfully generous Portuguese captain, one whom a less fresh-minded writer would have shown ill-treating him as belonging to an opposed nation and faith: instead the captain personifies the fellowship of humanity. It is not that Defoe takes a rosy view of mankind at large, but he does honestly recognise that kindness is as common as cruelty; straightforward decency is admitted in the true proportions of its occurrence.

Summaries · 21

The Sallee episode runs spiritedly, supplying all necessary points efficiently. Admittedly there are, not for the last time in the book, inconsistencies which doubtless result from hasty writing. Crusoe, for instance, is the solitary British captive, without fellowcountrymen to share his escape, yet the ship's carpenter of his Turkish master is, we hear, British, and the Moorish boy Xury has learnt English by 'conversing with us slaves'. Such little slips hardly impair the story's drive: worse is the nonchalance with which Crusoe admits he would have drowned Xury if necessary, and the readiness with which he sells him to the captain. Logically his explanation may hold water, that though 'loath to sell the poor boy's liberty' he considered Xury's own good: what better fate might Xury expect in Brazil than freedom after ten years serving a humane master? But one would like more signs of concern.

Crusoe's long coastal voyage before being rescued is less vividly described than the escape. Defoe has, roughly, two narrative manners; one is sharp, definitive, specific, and actual in detail—it creates a hallucinatory sense of immediate presentness (the sea-storms, relieving calm, encounter with the Turkish rover, slave life, and particulars of escape). Such things come across as real. The other manner is imprecise in image and sensation (mysterious African dangers, 'dreadful noises', 'vast creatures of many sorts [with] hideous howlings and yellings', and 'mighty creatures' plunging alarmingly in the sea). Steele's account of Alexander Selkirk likewise has 'Monsters of the Deep [whose] dreadful howlings and voices seemed too terrible ... for human ears'. To distinguish the realistic force in its stronger areas from the loose impressionism in its weaker is a good critical exercise.

NOTES AND GLOSSARY
vulgarly: commonly
Guinea: a region of West Africa
fore-mast man: sailor below officer rank
mess-mate: companion at meals
5 L.: five pounds weight
calenture: delirious tropical fever
rover of Sallee: pirate ship from Salé in Morocco
yards: horizontal spars across mast for holding sails
Canary Islands: off the shore of Morocco
bringing to: coming to a stop
athwart our quarter: opposite our side, towards the rear
half-pikes: short spears
powder-chests: wooden shot filled with powder and shrapnel
Maresco: Morisco, Moor, native of Morocco

hale home the main-sheet: pull the rope governing the mainsail
shoulder of mutton sail: triangular sail
the boom gibed: the spar for the sail swung from side to side
fuzees: fusil, light firearm
antient: ensign, flag
pendants: pennants, long narrow flags
case of bottles: wooden case of liquor bottles
bees-wax: wax secreted by bees, used as polishing or lighting material
twist: crotch, part of the body where legs fork
fowling-pieces: light guns for bird shooting
stretching to windward: keeping on towards the source of the wind
humane: human (not the modern sense of 'kind', 'merciful')
Cape de Verd Islands: off the coast of Senegal, West Africa
musquet-bore: capacity of a large hand-gun
slugs: bullets
Gambia or Senegall: rivers of the westernmost bulge of West Africa
admiration: astonishment
a large offing to make this point: well offshore to clear the headland
crowded: raised sails for speed
perspective-glasses: telescopes (also 'prospective-glasses')
a title: a tittle, the smallest detail
pieces of eight: old Spanish dollars
medium: compromise

Pages 55 to 60: from 'The generous treatment the captain gave me' to 'in order to act the rebel to their authority, and the fool to my own interest'.

This is an interlude before the fascinations of the island. From the Brazilian details, probably gathered from Dampier's pages (see p. 11), some noteworthy features emerge. One is, as before, the integrity of those among whom Crusoe falls, his Brazilian acquaintance, his English captain's generous widow, and the honest London merchant who provides for his trading. Far from melodramatising Crusoe's life in an alien land Defoe implies that diligence will be rewarded anywhere. He lodges Crusoe with 'a good honest man' who procures him a licence of settlement and sees him advancing rapidly to prosperity. A second noteworthy feature is the renewed tension, between the zest of practical success requiring perseverance (the pages rustle with activity, like the gust of healthy breezes) and on the other hand the urge to seek novelty and risk. Crusoe admits he is unreasonable; leaving home to seek fortune abroad, favoured by his abilities and honest partners he succeeds in exotic circumstances in South America. Yet he protests all he is achieving is the 'very middle station' rejected at home. This happens 'among strangers and savages in a wilderness' (sufficient challenge, surely, to an adventurer?) but drives him to lament that he never hears from England. Why then travel at all?

Unreasonable, yes. But obsessions drive him on, the 'obstinate adhering to my foolish inclination of wandering', allied now with a 'desire of rising faster than the nature of the thing admitted'. Yet still the air of enthusiastic practicality reigns; with the assurance of a business prospectus he outlines Guinea trade in terms of 'beads, toys, knives, scissors, bits of glass, and the like, not only gold dust, Guinea grains [spices, or drug seeds], elephants' teeth, &c., but negroes, for the service of the Brazils, in great numbers'. To this extent Crusoe is, as critics have called him, Economic Man. Yet his economics are those not of regular application but of exotic riskiness. Had he considered judiciously he would never have left 'all the probable views of a thriving circumstance, and gone upon a voyage to sea, attended with all its common hazards'. But 'I was hurried on, and obeyed blindly the dictates of my fancy rather than my reason'.

A strange sense of destiny overhangs this new venture. Inward compulsions drive him, and his sailing date proves to be the anniversary of the day he forsook his father to sail on his first voyage, and, moreover, of that when he fell captive to the Turks at Sallee. Later, the date when he is cast on the island proves to be his birthday: 'my wicked life [that before his conversion] and my solitary life begun both on a day'. Crusoe feels at the focus of mysterious powers.

NOTES AND GLOSSARY
letter of naturalization: grant of same rights as of a natural-born citizen
uncured: undeveloped
procuration: authorisation to act as deputy
consideration: recompense
bays: baize, coarse woollen cloth
grains: spices, or drug-seeds
engrossed in the publick: monopolised by an official agency
super-cargo: official supervising ship's cargo

Pages 61 to 76: from 'Our ship was about 120 tun burthen' to 'those things were of small use to me'.

The story from his leaving Brazil to his taking stock of the island opens admirably. The navigational details have the authenticity of true nautical journals yet are not too technical. (By contrast Swift, opening 'A Voyage to Brobdingnag' in *Gulliver's Travels* (1726), ruthlessly parodies seafaring jargon, borrowing closely from a contemporary seaman's manual.) The storm is described splendidly, with all Defoe's racy strength and speed; the prose moves with controlled intensity, in language at once clear and strenuous. The three paragraphs relating Crusoe's struggle in the sea are magnificent, beyond praise in their immediacy, vividness, and fullness of rendering, and as Crusoe clambers ashore they ring with a relief and thankfulness that sound absolutely true. By a stroke of psychological truth there follow the 'terrible agonies of mind' which come as he realises his real position. Amid this turmoil, rendered with circumstantial and dramatic fidelity, occurs that touch first praised by Sir Walter Scott, and seeming so intimate in its sense of loss—'I never saw them [his shipmates] afterwards, or any sign of them, except three of their hats, one cap, and two shoes that were not fellows'.

This instalment is short but works very powerfully. Apart from the unlikely touch that he was greatly refreshed by comfortable sleep all night in a thorny tree (his journal reveals further that it rained hard, too!), this is gripping narrative, packed with authenticating invention. The whole scene comes vividly across—the ship's situation, particulars of her stores, the raft-making, and the hazards of getting the salvage ashore. Each phrase conveys practical action or observation, impinging on the reader's attention as convincingly as on Crusoe's and with as immediate a sense of discovery, as, for instance, when he twice swims round the vessel before seeing that he has overlooked a short hanging rope, by which he clambers on deck. His resoluteness inspires the whole episode: 'it was in vain', he characteristically remarks, 'to sit still and wish for what was not to be had, and this extremity aroused my application.' (In *Farther Adventures* a Spanish castaway comments that his own countrymen 'should never have gotten half those things out of the ship as you did: Nay, says he, we should never have found means to have gotten a raft to carry them, ... and how much less should we have done, if any of us had been alone?')

Ostensibly the story is written, except for the journal, thirty years later, yet the effect is one of the immediate present. Everything, on ship and on the island, comes to the mind's eye freshly. 'To read *Robinson Crusoe*', James Sutherland observes, 'is to be compelled to face up to all sorts of physical problems that civilised man has long since forgotten. It is in some sense to retrace the history of the human race: it is certainly to look again with the eyes of childhood on many things that one has long since ceased to notice at all.' This dropping of scales from jaded eyes, this unexpected novelty of discovery or rediscovery, this freshness of assessment so that things strike with their true significance, is the book's special fascination. Much is unexpected, yet all is convincing, not least the famous and amusing moment when Crusoe first mocks the money he finds ('O drug!' said I aloud, 'what art thou good for?'), but then prudently pockets it, just in case of need. If the imagination's function is to make the new familiar, and the familiar new, this writing is brilliantly imaginative.

So Crusoe transfers from sea to land, and with the ship's destruction his last link is broken.

NOTES AND GLOSSARY
120 tun burthen: 120 tons carrying capacity
standing away: setting course
the height of Cape St. Augustino: the latitude of Cape St. Augustino, on the easternmost bulge of South America
Fernand de Noronha: northeast of Cape St. Augustino
past the line: crossed the Equator
coast of Guinea: modern Guiana, not the Guinea of earlier references
circle of the Carribee-Islands: the Caribbean Islands extend in a semi-circle northwards from South America.
indraft: inward flowing current
sprye: spray
breach of the sea: breaking of the waves
coup de grace: (*French*) final blow
clifts: cliffs
to shift me: to change my clothing
fore-chains: anchor chains at ship's bows
bulged: distorted so as to be no longer watertight
quarter: latter half
cordial waters: alcoholic or other stimulating drinks
rack: arrack, drink of fermented palm-juice or rice
powder-horns: gunpowder flasks
skrew-jack: hoisting device, worked by revolving handle
iron crows: crowbars, levers
fore-top-sail: sail set across upper mast
runlets: rundlets, small casks
hawser: large rope
spritsail-yard: pole under bowsprit for extending sail
missen-yard: mizzen-yard, pole for extending sail astern
gale: breeze (not the modern sense of 'tempest')
tide of flood: rising, flowing, tide

26 · Summaries

Pages 76 to 93: from 'My thoughts were now wholly employed' to 'I frequently found their nests, and got their young ones, which were very good meat'.

Crusoe starts accommodating himself to the island, making a shelter, securing his possessions, hunting wild goats. He never emulates Selkirk's prowess in catching these by swift running, but he shows his observant shrewdness by strategically stalking them from above rather than below. Much of the book's interest comes from his discovering strategies and processes, from devisings and adaptings. He safeguards his powder, shelves his cave, settles his programme, and hews his planks.

But with this, as he says, goes 'some little account of myself and of my thoughts about living'. Reflection sets him upon the self-scrutiny natural to any castaway but here resulting in a notable increase in insight. Defoe is concerned with Crusoe's moral evolution as well as his physical preservation. Prefacing *Serious Reflections* he claimed (rather questionably) that in *Robinson Crusoe* 'the fable is always made for the moral'—the story, that is, for the lesson. The main aim is certainly to grip the reader with fascinating adventures; yet the tradition of moral seriousness familiar to Defoe sought spiritual significances beneath material facts, and when the preface declares the story to be both historical and allegorical something is seen of his own dual life, external activities conjoined with Dissenter soul-searching. Actually, it was Gildon rather than Defoe who first hinted at covert autobiography in Robinson Crusoe; he imagined Defoe saying to the aggrieved Crusoe 'you are the true allegoric image of thy tender father D[anie]l; I drew thee from the consideration of my own mind: I have been all my life that rambling, inconsistent creature which I have made thee'. Defoe tacitly adopts this idea to imply that *Robinson Crusoe* is more than romantic yarning; it portrays a certain 'man alive, and well known too' (a man we naturally identify with Defoe himself, for whom moral reckonings were almost as essential as financial ones).

This section, then, starts the moral exploration so greatly developed later; the most explicit sign is the balance-sheet of 'Evil' and 'Good' circumstances which calls to his mind God's mercies.

NOTES AND GLOSSARY
adze: tool with blade curved at right-angle to the shaft
dubb: dub, make smooth
gudgeons: sockets
hodd: hod, V-shaped carrier for bricks or mortar
flaggs: flags, reeds

Pages 93 to 111: from 'And now, in the managing my household affairs' to 'they will find deliverance from sin a much greater blessing than deliverance from affliction'.

Physical and spiritual alternations develop further: Defoe keeps both dramatically alive. The first major step is the delightful episode of the unexpected grain-stalks, the seeming miracle of 'perfect green barley' which startles Crusoe into his first real sense of God's providence. This is beautifully told—the surprise, awe, thrilled speculation, and eventually commonplace solution which explodes the idea of miracle (though, Crusoe reflects, divine goodness is as evident in nature's regular bounties as in any supernatural interventions). Dissenters stressed the need for conversion and conviction, for the soul to awaken from lethargy to a certainty of God's power over it. This happens briefly to Crusoe, and though he relapses again the awakening has begun.

The shock of the earthquake and hurricane is grippingly conveyed. These are physical phenomena, and Crusoe is too startled for more than perfunctory prayer, yet their power symbolises a supernatural reality. There are probably echoes of the biblical story of Elijah the prophet, cast from his homeland into the wilderness, experiencing a violent wind and an earthquake, and then hearing God's voice. Defoe suggests no parallel, and any associations with Elijah are doubtless subconscious. Yet the episode alerts the reader forcefully, and Defoe implies a spiritual significance. Shortly after there follows the 'terrible dream' (linked with the storm and earthquake) presenting a supernatural visitant 'as bright as a flame': Elijah's storm and earthquake were also followed by a divine fire. Again the earth seems to quake, threatening Crusoe with death for unrepented sins.

The process of conversion then moves drastically forward. Hitherto even Crusoe's thankfulness at escaping drowning had ended merely in 'transports of the soul' which proved only a 'common flight of joy'. Now, increasingly jolted by the corn, earthquake, and vision, he feels the harrowing despair which afflicts the awakened soul. He accuses himself of 'uncommon wickedness', an hyperbole his actual story does not confirm, yet one habitually voiced by repentant sinners viewing their past lives.

Crusoe's crisis coincides with a severe ague-fit but that does not invalidate it; the sufferer needs to feel death near before being roused to the reality of hell or heaven. He has recourse then to his Bible, in which, as others had found, God's voice speaks directly to the awakened heart. Hitherto he has prayed only automatically. Now he prays 'with a sense of my condition and with a true scripture view of hope founded on the encouragement of the word of God'. This whole phase — corn/earthquake/vision/terror/prayer/repentance/reverence — is movingly passionate. Whether Defoe experienced its parallel we can only guess, but either through his own crisis or through imaginative sympathy with the recorded experiences of others he brings his account to a striking height of conviction.

NOTES AND GLOSSARY

oakum: strands of tarred rope
blowing tide: rising, flowing, tide
case bottle: bottle protected by a wooden holder
children of Israel: the biblical book of Psalms relates that the Jews, wandering in the wilderness, complained in the words Defoe quotes that God was letting them starve
my well day of course: the day I was well in the natural course of things (agues are intermittent diseases)
brand goose: brent goose, small wild goose

Pages 111 to 126: from 'But leaving this part, I return to my journal' to 'assisting me afterwards to save it out of the wreck of the ship'.

By emotional convalescence, as it were, a quieter series of island interests follows. Supported by religious 'comfort within', Crusoe surveys his island, observes its 'pleasant savannas or meadows', and finds plentiful melons and grapes and 'a constant verdure or flourish of spring'. Obeying his new religious allegiance he notches up the Sabbath days on his pole: all this is very like Selkirk's experience. He devoutly commemorates the anniversary of his landing; he records the seasons, tries basket-weaving, finds abundant turtles and wildfowl, and captures a kid to start a herd of goats. He responds amiably to companionable animals, as the delightful passages with his parrot show, a trait perhaps drawn from Selkirk's singing and dancing before his goats and cats. All in all, Crusoe settles comfortably in his stockade, lord of his lands; we growingly sense this intimacy and familiarisation.

His relatively comfortable situation does not prevent occasional revulsions from the island and yearnings for company, hinting forward to Friday's appearance. Again, though professedly writing years later, Crusoe captures an immediate sense of fluctuating emotions; the two paragraphs contrasting his misery and joy throb with the eloquence of true feeling (they begin 'Before, as I walked about' and 'But now I began to exercise myself'). And the two which follow, honestly questioning the nature of his contentment, are convincingly right.

Summaries · 29

NOTES AND GLOSSARY
cassava: tapioca
alloes: aloes, shrubs producing a bitter drug
raisins of the sun: sun-dried grapes
Leaden-hall Market: London's main meat market
hutch: shed, shelter
a meer domestick: a veritable inmate of the house

Pages 126 to 146: from 'Thus, and in this disposition of mind' to 'better than the utmost enjoyment of human society in the world'.

Crusoe is now, on the whole, temperamentally attuned to the island, and it is time for further practical enterprises: alternations of inward and outward life keep him moving before us. A considerable section follows in which his resourcefulness—described in *Serious Reflections* as 'indefatigable application and undaunted resolution under the greatest and most discouraging circumstances'—tackles plank-hewing (Dampier tells of South American natives doing likewise), the growing and reaping of crops, and 'the strange multitude of little things necessary to the providing, producing, curing, dressing, making, and finishing this one article of bread': how much, one is reminded, social life is eased by the division of labour. He teaches Poll to speak ('the first word I ever heard spoken in the island by any mouth but my own'), and he makes pots, an operation doubtless given its extraordinary vividness by Defoe's experience of tile-making at Tilbury.

    Though ardent in such activities, however, Crusoe has strong impulses to escape. To their obsessive nature is due, presumably, his blindness to the danger of reaching a hostile shore. Earlier he surmised that the mainland might be 'all inhabited by savages', yet here he disregards such danger, a sign, Defoe might say, not of author's negligence but of obsessional blindness. Another such blindness persuades him that hewing a tree to make 'a canoe, or periagua' (an echo probably of Dampier's 'pereagoes or canoes') will be easy. A third is his making the craft too heavy and too far from water, even though already he has been similarly disappointed at failing to shift the stranded lifeboat. Realistically, all three stupidities are unlikely; no one would overlook the danger of savages, or the problem of managing an enormous canoe; but Defoe tries to avert scepticism by blaming these oversights on Crusoe's frenzy of desire ('most like a fool'). Realistically they are unconvincing, but they reflect that side of Crusoe which volcanic urges thrust up. And so, with the picturesque account of his shaggy clothes and umbrella which from childhood is every reader's picture of him, Crusoe ends his fourth year on the significant reflection that his religious comfort supports him 'better than the utmost enjoyment of human society'.

NOTES AND GLOSSARY
bows: boughs
half a peck: a gallon
sensibly: feelingly
wooden manner: dull, stupid fashion
pipkins: earthenware pots
upon the whole: all in all
cedar tree ... Solomon: when Solomon, King of the Jews in the Bible, built a temple to God, he commanded that cedars should be brought from the neighbouring land of Lebanon for its construction
grutches: grudges
flea: flay, take skin off
Elijah ... ravens: the prophet Elijah, in the Bible, having denounced Israel's King Ahab, was sent by God into the wilderness for safety, and there fed by ravens
chequered: patterned in varied colours
equinox: equator (probably Defoe's slip)
indifferently well: reasonably well, satisfactorily

Pages 146 to 162: from 'I cannot say that after this, for five years, any extraordinary thing happened to me' to 'But now I come to a new scene of my life'.

Hereabouts the story might have dropped into routine: instead it maintains its drive with a series of lively happenings. The first, powerfully told, is that of the current which all but sweeps Crusoe away. Lest a sceptic doubt whether tidal races occur in the open ocean Defoe later explains it as 'the great draft and reflux of the mighty Oroonoko' since he heeds detail better than critics often recognise. The rushing water makes Crusoe's first canoe trip shockingly dangerous and the whole affair is grippingly told: the technical explanation of the currents and their interacting swirls which eventually deliver him back to safety, exhausted, is clear and strong, and Crusoe's terror is finely communicated. Once more Defoe proves a master of drama; nowhere is the story more compellingly alive.

It then moves to domestic pleasures—the companionable parrot, the soothing homemade tobacco pipe ('a very ugly clumsy thing'), the management of his goats, the setting up of his dairy, the comedy of his absolute sovereignty, and the ludicrousness of his appearance. There is a warmth of intimacy and comforting familiarity, and the charm of this shows itself if Crusoe's island life is compared with his wide post-island wanderings in *Farther Adventures* (which admittedly few readers tackle). The events of *Robinson Crusoe* familiarise us, like Crusoe, with a place which comes to feel like home, a setting for ordered, coherent life in which the confidence of belonging makes psychological sense. By contrast the events of *Farther Adventures*, in ever-varying environments, exciting though they are, produce a sense of shapeless transience, even meaninglessness.

These pages yield their full quality only on reflection. Prefaced by the horror of ocean helplessness and by devout gratitude for escape, they form a pastoral oasis of benign amenity before the famous crisis of the human footstep. Defoe constructs instinctively rather than deliberately, and indeed, like Crusoe's life, the book goes along freely and chancily. Yet strong alternations of fortune are central to its management, and these companionable pages lead to what follows by fine instinct for dramatic form. 'Now', Crusoe proclaims, 'I come to a new scene of my life.'

NOTES AND GLOSSARY

terra firma:	dry land
step:	lodging, socket, for end of pole
graplin:	grapling, grapnel, small anchor
frigate:	medium-sized warship (here jocular)
drills:	rills, streams
crazy:	enfeebled
spatter-dashes:	leggings
frog:	loop hanging from belt, for carrying weapon
moletta:	mulatto, of mixed white and negro parentage
physical:	good for health

Pages 162 to 181: from 'It happened one day about noon' to 'I had not the least notion of any such thing depending, or the least supposition of it being possible'.

The new scene opens with the sight of the footprint. This stamps itself on the mind with almost surrealistic shock. In reality, a single footprint, though not impossible, is an extremely unlikely phenomenon since it would require all the seashore to be bone-hard save for one tiny patch. But artistically, in its shattering distinctness, the effect is perfect.

Crusoe's delusively calm satisfactions vanish before flight and terrified brooding, and one appreciates how dramatic is the contrast with what has preceded. In 'The Question of Emotion in Defoe' (included in *Daniel Defoe: a Collection of Critical Essays*, edited by Max Byrd, 1976) Benjamin Boyce rejects the stereotype of an unimpassioned Defoe or phlegmatic Crusoe: 'Crusoe ... at this point becomes another symbolic figure [already having symbolised the stranger in a strange world], the man whose laboriously and painfully acquired self-confidence in the difficult world is threatened by new conditions, new enemies ... This book, in its central, famous part, is loaded with fear.' Crusoe indeed, except at moments, is far from phlegmatic: in emotive situations emotion is what he feels. Here he feels it sensationally.

An oddity occurs as he wonders; could Satan himself have caused the footprint?—an idea suggesting that Crusoe is a naive religious traditionalist. He rejects this notion in favour of 'some more dangerous creature', a visiting savage, as the agent. More dangerous than Satan? Crusoe's mind does a curious straddle. One part believes in a literal Devil, capable of physical manifestations, but another part reduces this terrible being to a conventional figment. A little later he sees two eyes shining from a black cave, 'whether man or devil I knew not', and he valiantly reflects that 'he that was afraid to see the devil was not fit to live twenty years in an island all alone'. Defoe's ideas are ancient and modern: in seventeenth-century style Crusoe could believe in the personal physical agency of the Devil; in eighteenth-century style a rational explanation is infinitely likelier—actual savages are a far greater threat to him than the supposed but remote great enemy of mankind.

At any rate, natural as is the cause of Crusoe's alarm, his fear develops strongly, even extravagantly. He stays indoors three days, hysterically plans how to hide without trace, builds his defences ten feet thick, plants nearly twenty thousand screening trees, lives two years expecting always to be murdered, and 'night and day' broods on how to slaughter invaders.

This is overwrought sensationalism. Yet, to close this phase, reason intervenes. In a striking reflective analysis Crusoe comes to be a moral relativist (as thinkers in Defoe's time increasingly became), viewing moral customs not by pre-established absolutes but in relation to conditioning circumstances. Cannibalism naturally horrifies him, but the very depth of his horror makes the more impressive his change of view. 'I was', he concludes, 'certainly in the wrong of it ... I was perfectly out of my duty when I was laying all my bloody schemes for the destruction of innocent people.' The cannibals are 'innocent' because they have not harmed him. God has chosen not to enlighten them, and their cannibalism results from natural conditions. So, after its initial shock, this powerful episode reaches a stabilising, thoughtful end.

NOTES AND GLOSSARY
amusement: bewilderment
stated inhabitants: settled residents
the main: the open sea
cutlash: cutlass, short broad sword
signals: signs, traces
pretend: claim, assume the right
they were national: they pertained to the national customs
chop'd: chanced, come suddenly

Pages 181 to 187: from 'This renewed a contemplation which often had come to my thoughts' to 'my last years of solitary residence in this island'.

This is a peaceable lull before strong drama. It starts reflecting impressively on those 'secret hints and pressings' of mind by which God seeks to sway his creatures away from selfwill and towards his intentions. These are really an essay on conscience, the pull which prefers selfless good to selfish desire and speaks of divine guidance: *Robinson Crusoe* is closer to the manner of *Serious Reflections* than is often recognised. Crusoe's 'secret intimations' are, however, more mysterious than conscience. Conscience can give moral reasons for its promptings, whereas Crusoe's 'hints' seem unaccountable, though certainly they are taken to come from God.

Some amiable pages follow, about candle-making, companionship with his pets, and general placidity, but only as a prelude to violent alarms, which nevertheless herald Crusoe's ultimate deliverance. On this momentous note the interlude ends.

NOTES AND GLOSSARY
meer natural cave: entirely natural cave
twelve foot over: twelve foot across
wild-fire: explosive matter
pan: part of gun which holds gunpowder for ignition
capitulated: come to terms

34 · Summaries

Pages 187 to 204: from 'It was now the month of December' to 'no savages came near me for a great while'.

This section moves towards crisis. First, seeing cannibals on his own side of the island, Crusoe plunges into a murderous temper despite his theoretical tolerance; he is a man of strong variable moods. His perturbation, with 'frightful dreams', lasts an improbable fifteen months until one day he hears gunfire from a ship wrecked on the reef past which currents had almost swept him away. Since no one survives, the thought of lost companions causes a passionate yearning finely conveyed in phrases which urge themselves rhythmically onward in simple natural poetry:

> I cannot explain by any possible energy of words what a strange longing or hankering of desires I felt in my soul upon this sight; breaking out sometimes thus: 'O that there had been but one or two; nay, or but one soul saved out of this ship, to have escaped to me, that I might but have had one companion, one fellow-creature to have spoken to me, and to have conversed with!' In all the time of my solitary life, I never felt so earnest, so strong a desire after the society of my fellow-creatures, or so deep a regret at the want of it ... I believe I repeated the words 'O that it had been but one!' a thousand times, and the desires were so moved by it, that when I spoke the words my hands would clinch together, and my fingers press the palms of my hands, that if I had had any soft thing in my hand, it would have crushed it involuntarily; and my teeth in my head would strike together, and set against one another so strong, that for some time I could not part them again.

The reader feels right through the words to the heartache.

An impulse from 'some invisible direction' prompts Crusoe to explore the wreck, an exploration graphically described, and made moving by the distressed dog and drowned sailors. We follow him from item to item with ever-fresh sense of discovery; then the excitement subsides into another domestic lull.

Yet the thought of lost companions haunts him; his restiveness returns and his 'unlucky head' is agitated. By 'head' he means not rational intellect but headstrongness, and this causes him further reflection on his 'original sin' of wilfulness. Throughout, *Robinson Crusoe* humanises its story by interplaying successive emotions—here, the awakened yearning for companions, the practical excitements of the wreck, the quiet interlude, the resurgence of desire.

What follows is particularly tense, as though an electrical charge were mounting. Crusoe's agitation ('the innumerable crowd of thoughts that whirled through that great thorow-fare of the brain'), his review of his experience, his recognition of how narrowly safety approaches disaster, and his feverish reckoning of chances for escape—these so approach psychological crisis as to be 'the fruit of a disturbed mind, an impatient temper, made as it were desperate'. Far from being the imperturbable stoic, Crusoe suffers acute temperamental fluctuations. His prized religious stability collapses before an irresistible 'impetuosity of desire' to escape. He dreams a premonitory dream of a rescued savage and prospects of freedom, and awakes dejectedly to isolation, but resolves to face whatever may come.

NOTES AND GLOSSARY
naturalists: natural scientists
boltsprit: bowsprit, spar extending forward from ship's bow
head: foremost part of ship
doubloons: old Spanish gold coins
glazed powder: gunpowder and graphite mixed, for greater safety
ryals: reals, small Spanish silver coins
if I had ever escaped: if I should ever escape
moydors: moidores, Portuguese gold coins
even all the while: actually the whole time
upon the scout: on the lookout

Pages 204 to 230: from 'About a year and a half after I had entertained these notions' to 'nobody cared to stir abroad, either by land or sea'.

The climax comes quickly, with Friday's rescue. The spirited narrative is alive in its breathless speed and what it means to both men—the chase, the impetuous movements, the surprises. Friday proves a fine, comely fellow (his 'bright kind of dun olive colour' is 'not very easy to describe', Crusoe admits, but the phrase is a commendable shot at precise rendering, meaning presumably some darkish yet glowing soft honey shade). Friday's merits are as agreeable as is Crusoe's joy in his company; they prompt questions why, since non-Christians often outdo Christians in virtue, God has withheld from them, indeed from most of mankind, the keys to salvation, as Christians used to believe.

This question was posing itself increasingly as wider knowledge of the world revealed differing cultures and faiths. Pope wrote a poem, 'The Universal Prayer' (or 'The Deist's Hymn'), praising a God 'In ev'ry Clime ador'd / By Saint, by Savage, and by Sage', and rejecting the traditional Christian arrogance of believing all non-Christians damned. Fielding's novel *Joseph Andrews* (1742) has its charitable Parson Adams tell the uncharitable Parson Barnabas that God prefers the virtuous heathen to the vicious Christian, no matter how orthodox the latter's faith. Crusoe wonders why non-Christians should be thought unqualified for salvation and concludes, not very satisfactorily, that if non-Christians are doomed this must be for sinning against their own best lights, and that an all-wise God should not be criticised for edicts which ignorant man cannot comprehend.

Crusoe is a man of normal good sense and reason, not outstandingly intellectual. His questions show a mind decently open, even if his conclusions half-close it again (and many trained theologians did no better). At any rate, his dealings with Friday are heartwarming and fulfil a deep human need (though later, briefly, he inexcusably distrusts Friday's loyalty should he rejoin his own tribe, and even fears he might relish eating him). Friday's readiness with English is unlikely even though, says Crusoe, 'he was the aptest scholar that ever was': the satirical Gildon portrayed him complaining to Crusoe that the latter taught him English 'tolerably well' at first but left him no better twelve years later. This, though, the story's briskness makes the reader cheerfully swallow.

Converts to a cause, like Crusoe, often feel bound to pass their newfound faith on to others. A French priest in *Farther Adventures* makes the point: 'True religion is naturally communicative, and he that is once made a Christian will never leave a pagan behind him if he can help it.' So Crusoe gets to work upon Friday and soon faces doctrinal problems with which, he honestly confesses, he finds it salutary though difficult to struggle. The lifeline he seizes is one increasingly grasped by undoctrinaire Christians of Defoe's day, that Christianity needs plain acceptance of the Bible as interpreted by the reverent, undisputatious human heart, 'and this without any teacher or instructor'. Crusoe and Friday discover what seventeenth-century violences had slowly taught England, that 'all the disputes, wranglings, strife, and contention which has happened in the world about religion ... were all perfectly useless'. So things proceed lovingly between the two, as they make a boat together, until the next crisis, the last cannibal incursion.

NOTES AND GLOSSARY
clapped: thrust
hallowing: hallooing, calling out
as cleaverly: as expertly as a butcher using his cleaver (with a probable pun on 'cleverly')

Summaries · 37

sensibly surprized: perceptibly startled
admired: wondered at
learned him: taught him (an out-of-date usage)
to relish with me: to please my taste
I was not wanting: I did not neglect
doctor: teacher, scholar
affectionately: feelingly
Mediator of the new covenant: Jesus, as expounder of the new message of God's forgiveness and mercy to mankind
the redemption of man by the Saviour: Christian doctrine holds that through the merits and self-sacrifice of Jesus Christ believers are saved from punishment for their sins
seed of Abraham: human form, as a descendent of Abraham (the earliest and greatest Jewish patriarch in the Bible)
more affection: deeper feelings
comfortable views: strengthening ideas
hanger: short sword
study'd upon: pondered over
dull: despondent, downcast
fustic: tropical American tree; its wood gives a yellow dye
Nicaragua wood: tropical American tree; its wood gives a red dye
rowlers: rollers
boom: pole along which lower edge of sail is extended
stay: rope supporting mast

Pages 230 to 247: from 'I was now entered on the seven and twentieth year' to 'I found I had kept a true reckoning of years'.

The rescue of the Spanish captain and Friday's father brings out Defoe's most effective qualities. Crisp phrases, moment by moment, speed the story along. Friday's participation spreads the interest more broadly than before, as does that of the Spaniard; yet every detail remains clear, every movement precisely timed. After action, emotion: Friday's unexpected reunion with his father is deeply touching, evidence again of Defoe's skill at emotional variation, an extension of companionship which enriches one's sense of what being warmly human means. Happiness and heartfelt relief sound in every phrase. Yet the story escapes sentimental indulgence; it is sustained by practical details (the plans and requirements for rescuing the other shipwrecked Spaniards and Portuguese), and enlivened by very spirited writing.

Consider, as displaying these qualities, the five paragraphs about receiving the castaways, beginning 'Having now society enough, and

38 · Summaries

our number being sufficient' and ending 'that indeed was a question we never asked'. What impresses is the sense of companionable effort and shared anticipation. Far from merely recording actions, the writing re-enacts, explains, foresees, evaluates, and communicates so amply that it seems more like dialogue than monologue. Crusoe is the sole narrator, yet his words hum with a beehive-like zest of co-operation; a sense of mutual participation unites him to his fellows and all of them to us. This captivating sense of involvement is the main reason why, from the first, *Robinson Crusoe* has proved so compellingly readable. As these paragraphs end, there is the straight-faced comedy of the written guarantees of loyalty to be required from castaways known to lack pen and ink. Crusoe's enterprises, now he has friends to share them with, take on an aspect of game.

You should analyse the narrative skill with which Defoe relates the rescues in these sections.

NOTES AND GLOSSARY
swan-shot: large-sized shot
cock and present: prepare to pull gun's trigger and take aim
bad Friday do so: ordered Friday to do so
defaced: removed traces of
New Spain: Spanish colonies in South America
Inquisition: Roman Catholic office for suppression of heresy
children of Israel ... wilderness: the Israelites, freed from slavery in Egypt, made their way towards their promised home but suffered hardships in the desert
Alicant: a district of southern Spain
magazine: storehouse
firelock: gun fired by a lock with flint and steel
good husbands: careful, thrifty, managers

Pages 247 to 274: from 'Under these instructions, the Spaniard and the old savage' to 'I arrived in England, the eleventh of June, in the year 1687, having been thirty and five years absent'.

The story now approaches its end. Protected by divine guidance Crusoe feels 'secret hints and notices of danger' as a longboat comes ashore from an English ship. A vigorous touch-and-go adventure follows as the mutineers are outwitted in strategies both businesslike and ingenious. Defoe manages it all with unflagging intentness and fine skill in keeping everything sharply definite, until the climax is reached when Crusoe not only scores total victory but finds himself, by the captain's gratitude, the rescued ship's owner for the time being. In one lucid, firm, sentence he records how all his hopes come true, and the simplicity of statement has a classical finality about it:

> I cast my eyes to the ship, and there she rode within little more than half a mile of the shore; for they had weighed her anchor as soon as they were masters of her; and the weather being fair, had brought her to an anchor just against the mouth of the little creek; and the tide being up, the captain had brought the pinnace in near the place where I at first landed my rafts, and so landed just at my door.

The wheel, from first casting ashore to final deliverance, has come full circle. Do we sense an implicit tremor of nostalgia when he mentions the little creek, around which so much of his island life has revolved? This is where it all happened, the practical struggles, the home-making in exile, the religious musings; all that Crusoe has done combines in a sense of belongingness, despite his occasional urges to escape. Compared with Defoe's more itinerant stories, *Robinson Crusoe* gets enrichment from experience accumulating in one place. As Crusoe is rescued, there is a reticent poignancy when the rescuing vessel anchors at a spot he knows so well, and the pinnace lands just where, so long ago, he had with such difficulty grounded the raft and cargo by which he survived.

The simplicity of style hereabouts is fine natural art. The outbreak of feelings immediately following is heartfelt reaction at having lived through so much, and a lucid eloquence rings through Crusoe's gratitude for 'testimonies we had of a secret hand of Providence governing the world'. Then, sturdily refocussing his attention, he exults in 'six large bottles of Madeira wine', 'two pound of excellent good tobacco', and supplies of food and clothes. After the religious rapture this returns us appreciatively to earth: the rescued solitary deserves his pendulum-swing back to comfort.

So, after summary punishment of the mutineers, Crusoe takes 'my parrot' (presumably not—unless Defoe blundered—Poll, earlier said to be left behind) and the 'useless' money he has sensibly hoarded, and in a brief factual paragraph sails away on another significant anniversary, that of his Sallee escape nearly forty years earlier. His life, he implies, runs to some mysterious plan.

It is well worth carefully studying the interplay of action and feeling in this crucial phase.

NOTES AND GLOSSARY
ousy: oozy
reduced: subdued, brought back to obedience
bisket: biscuit

40 · Summaries

Leeward Islands: island group in the Caribbean Sea
fleet: float
particularly: even (an unusual usage)
amused: befooled, bewildered
imprecations: religious vows (an obsolete usage)
quarter decks: upper decks between stern and aftermast
round-house: cabin on the quarter deck
yard-arm: end of the main yard (the main beam supporting sails)
weigh: raise anchor
pickled: sluiced with brine and vinegar after flogging
barco-longo: low open vessel

Pages 274 to 299: from 'When I came to England' to the end.

There follow two main interests. One is how Crusoe handles personal and business matters, the other how he crosses the Pyrenees. Neither needs long comment. On the personal side he seems singularly cool: if in his religious redemption there is a Prodigal-Son analogy, in his family dealings there is none. On meeting his sisters and nephews his only reaction is to observe that, having been presumed dead, he gets nothing from the family estate; then, in three lines of the next-to-last page, he marries ('and that not either to my disadvantage or dissatisfaction'—how cordial a tribute!), has three children, and loses his wife: he then departs for the East Indies. (In *Farther Adventures*, however,—though that work hardly affects *Robinson Crusoe*—he claims to be much attached to a loving wife so that, resisting his longing for further travel, he lives 'a kind of heavenly life' in the country until her sudden death renews his obsession. He then entrusts his children to his good widow friend and goes abroad.)

With business associates he manages better. They treat him with admirable honesty—the ship's owners, the Portuguese captain in Lisbon, the Brazilian administrators—and Crusoe responds generously, not forgetting the 'poor widow, whose husband had been my first benefactor'. His two sisters also meet a warmer response than at first; each receives £100. It is, after all, rather a decent world.

The Pyrenean adventure looks like a device for filling the volume out. It is lightweight entertainment, making Friday improbably familiar with wolves and bears (his native land actually has none); nevertheless, he tackles this particular bear divertingly, and every instant of the exploit stands vividly out. The episode of the wolves, too, has sensational gusto. But none of this is more than amusement: whereas the island was the setting for the protracted, many-levelled testing of the spirit, the Pyrenean transit is lively anecdote.

So concludes 'the first part of a life of fortune and adventure, a life of Providence's chequer-work'—a life more magnetically readable than, probably, any other that fiction can offer.

NOTES AND GLOSSARY
procurator fiscal: legal financial authority
molossus: molasses, sugarcane treacle
moidores: Portuguese gold coins
straiten: put into difficulties
cruisadoes: crusados, Portuguese coins marked with a cross
Ave Marias: form of prayer in Roman Catholic Christianity
the latter end of Job: the restored prosperity of Job, a patriarch in the Bible, after years of affliction
the Start near Torbay: headland and bay in south-west England
the Groyne: Corunna, or La Coruna, in north-west Spain
Bay of Biscay: the bay bordered by Spain and France
Rochell: La Rochelle in western France
Calais ... Dover: French and English ports on the English Channel
Navarre: province of north-east Spain, bordering France
Pampeluna: Pamplona, in Navarre
Old Castile: formerly a central province of Spain
Fonterabia: Fuentarrabia, on the Spanish-French border
Bourdeaux: Bordeaux, in south-west France
Languedoc: province of south-west France
Gascoign: Gascony, province of south-west France, bordering Spain
nice: over-particular, hard to please
rankling: festering
Thoulouse: Toulouse, in south-west France
center of my travels: goal of my journeyings
bark: small sailing vessel

Part 3

Commentary

THE MAIN POINTERS to the nature, purpose, and achievement of *Robinson Crusoe*, already mentioned incidentally, now need more methodical development. That is the aim of this section.

What sort of novel?

The panorama Defoe spreads before us is so readily acceptable that no complicated analysis seems needed to grasp its features: criticism of *Robinson Crusoe* often becomes straightforward description of its contents and manner. Apparently unaware that he is launching a great literary form, Defoe achieves his masterpiece by what seems unthinking conjunction of travellers' tales, journalists' readableness, and the instinct for novelty. To quote Coleridge again, 'our imagination is kept in full play, excited to the highest, yet all the while we are touching or touched by common flesh and blood'. It seems simple, and in essence it is.

To have a masterpiece so accessible is of first-rate importance. Recently, in a BBC interview, one of Britain's best contemporary novelists, John Fowles, objected to writers who aim merely at a sophisticated public. What has gone wrong with the novel, he argued, is 'the notion that the novelist has to write for an intellectual élite. If you *can* write for a wide audience, then you *ought* to'. 'Most of all', he continued, 'I admire Defoe for his readability, the way he urges you on through the story.' Defoe's life and style belonged not with any élite but with the workaday 'middle state': 'more than most authors, Defoe had *lived*', as Pat Rogers remarks in his excellent 'Critical Heritage' volume of Defoe criticism (1972). So directly does *Robinson Crusoe* reproduce real life that we need alert attention before appreciating this apparent transcript for the creative thing it is. If there is an 'art of fiction' here is it more than primitive, direct, story-telling? 'Defoe is surely unique', Pat Rogers goes on, 'in the delays he experienced before being permitted to arrive as a serious artist', as more than Leslie Stephen's 'narrator of plain facts' and 'reporter minus the veracity'.

It is to this very fact—that it seems not art but nature touching 'common flesh and blood'—that *Robinson Crusoe* owes its universality. Within its first four months (April-July 1719) it had six printings of a thousand copies each. English editions have been almost innumerable, and in *The Imaginary Voyage in Prose Fiction* (1941) P.B. Gove lists an astonishing variety of foreign versions; in Germany there is even a term for the whole category of imitations, the 'Robinsonade'. Yet because *Robinson Crusoe* seems so artless the credit of establishing the novel as a literary form often goes instead to Richardson's *Pamela* (1740) and its offshoot, Fielding's *Joseph Andrews* (1742), with their evidence of authorial control. It is true that, as Pat Rogers says, 'Defoe was instinctively felt to be a great novelist long before the equipment existed to show why he was one', but this feeling did not set him up as the fountainhead of any great tradition.

His art, though, is not less striking for being inconspicuous. The story is not uncoloured, unselected fact but fact dramatised through Crusoe (whose character will be examined shortly). What we have is human tension, observation, and experience, and these humanise the mechanics of action. To say that is to say that the novel has arrived, for that is the novel's fundamental way.

But how does *Robinson Crusoe* make its particular effect? Its style will be discussed later; here let us examine how it imposes its invented world upon the imagination. Though any generalisation admits of exceptions, the specific nature of novels is to gain the reader's assent by presenting likely actions from convincing motives in a realistic setting. 'Its province', Dr Johnson commented, 'is to bring about natural events by easy means . . . ; it is therefore precluded from the machines and expedients of the heroic romance, and can neither employ giants to snatch away a lady from the nuptial rites, nor knights to bring her back from captivity.'

From the start, Crusoe might well be a real person: dates, circumstances, and discussions are absolutely lifelike. The point needs no labouring; everywhere the particulars of shiplife, cargoes, routes, details of work and topography and daily resource, and renderings of thoughts and moods, are specific and convincing. For a novelist merely to list particulars would not automatically produce so vivid a result; that comes from the way the facts are related through Crusoe's perceptions. Because Crusoe is so credible we sense things as he himself does, through his own responses, whether these are soberly practical, eagerly experimental, or tense with hope or dread. Crusoe not only perceives his circumstances, he experiences them. The following passage (p.257: from Crusoe's scheme for outwitting the mutineers) looks like mere factual travel-adventure narrative, yet note how full it is of dramatic attentiveness:

> I told him [the captain] the first thing we had to do was to stave the boat which lay upon the beach, so that they [the mutineers] might not carry her off; and taking everything out of her, leave her so far useless as not to be fit to swim [float]: accordingly we went on board, took the arms which were left on board out of her, and whatever else we found there, which was a bottle of brandy, and another of rum, a few bisket cakes, a horn of powder, and a great lump of sugar in a piece of canvas; the sugar was five or six pounds; all which was very welcome to me, especially the brandy and sugar, of which I had had none left for many years.
>
> When we had carried all these things on shore (the oars, mast, sail, and rudder of the boat were carried away before, as above) we knocked a great hole in her bottom, that if they had come strong enough to master us, yet they could not carry off the boat.
>
> Indeed, it was not much in my thoughts that we could be able to recover the ship; but my view was that if they went away without the boat, I did not much question to make her fit again, to carry us away to the Leeward Islands, and call upon our friends, the Spaniards, in my way, for I had them still in my thoughts.

Crusoe's mind plays around everything in a running dialogue with his circumstances. Past actions, future possibilities, other participants, all are actively real, and even amidst schemes for survival he is eagerly interested in the goods he finds aboard. Defoe's characters ignore the aesthetics of experience; as Taine observes, 'the idea of the beautiful never enters'. But they respond briskly to things, and from Crusoe's mere mention of prosaic articles and practical plans there arise an appreciative recognition and gratified eagerness which the spare, non-literary language brings directly across.

So we share Crusoe's reactions, and are always with him in all he experiences: 'the situation', in Sir Walter Scott's words, 'is such as every man may make his own', and this is because the facts are convincing and an alert attentiveness relates them to us. A 'narrator of plain facts' would give merely a fraction of what Crusoe gives as he explores the wreck, or establishes his 'castle', stalks wild goats, grows barley and rice, makes utensils and clothes himself, and so on. Our hearts rise with his successes and sink with his failures. To quote Taine again 'Never was such a sense of the real before or since. Our realists of today, painters, anatomists, decidedly men of business, are far from his naturalness: art and calculation crop out amidst their too minute descriptions. Defoe creates illusion.'

Robinson Crusoe indeed extends further, beyond facts or even character-drama; a further reflection of Taine's suggests the quality which makes it one of the world's archetypal stories, uniting practical adventure narrative and a fundamental vision of human potential:

> In this disposition of mind there is nothing a man cannot endure or do. Heart and hand come to the assistance of the arms; religion consecrates labour, piety feeds patience; and man, supported on one side by his instincts, on the other by his beliefs, finds himself able to clear the land, to people, to organise, and to civilise continents.

Robinson Crusoe not only tells an exciting story but conveys a major sense of mankind and the world: mobilising all his faculties, Crusoe turns accidents into constructive form, and personifies human resilience at large.

What other qualities make this a major novel? Though its form is loose, within that form Defoe tells excellent episodic stories; scene after scene stands out memorably, focussed on exactly those details (including unexpected ones) which would strike one in real life, and presented with such effective timing as carries expectation spiritedly forward—the Yarmouth voyage, Sallee escape, shipwreck and salvage, ague attack and dream, barley raising, ocean peril, footprint, Spanish wreck, Friday's rescue, and the like. Repeatedly Defoe shows a masterly instinct for the living rhythm of action. The storm which wrecks Crusoe's ship and hurls him into the surf to struggle ashore is magnificent in its sense of natural force and human striving. Equally fine is the throbbing excitement of Friday's rescue, or later of his father's and the Spanish captain's escape, or the recovery of the English ship.

Though such narrative triumphs occur, it would seem, unplanned, yet an instinctive phasing varies the story's appeal. Physical thrills alternate with mental musings, dramatic struggles with pastoral reflections. New interests come well-spaced; there is always a sense of discovery, of unforeseen turns which still are quite natural. From an assured 'middle state' Crusoe courts risk and danger: setting up for a Guinea trader he suffers 'the surprising change ... from a merchant to a miserable slave': settling into steady island life and religious assurance he is terrified by the footprint, and his confidence in God's protection vanishes. Thus does 'Providence's chequer-work' show itself in dramatic shifts and changes.

His restlessness—'the general plague of mankind'—repeatedly stirs the story into action. It is a strength of the book that Crusoe is much the 'rambling, inconsistent creature' Gildon satirically saw in Defoe. 'Rambling' and 'inconsistent' Crusoe may be, but within very human limits; his varying moods are essential to his book's dynamics, and the drama of differing tones, pressures, and speeds gives it its vitality. Not only are its adventures (as the title-page proclaims) strange and surprising; new facets and contrasts of experience are always interplaying. The tale, like life, moves by impulsive phases.

Sometimes, though, writing for popular tastes Defoe heightens an effect into improbability. The African monsters melodramatically howling from the shore have already been mentioned, as has the unlikelihood that even an exhausted castaway would awake refreshed from a rainy night in a thorny tree. Crusoe would hardly be 'almost frighted with two or three seals' or, unable to move a stranded boat, tackle a tree six feet in diameter to make a canoe or, failing in that and having made a smaller canoe, dig a canal six feet wide, four feet deep, and half a mile long to float it (a superhuman task) or, however alarmed by a strange footprint, make his defensive wall 'above ten feet thick'. Nor, conceivably, would he be so scared as not to 'peep abroad' for three days or, after seeing evidence of the cannibals' feast, keep 'close within [his] own circle for almost two years' and brood 'night and day' how to kill them, or feel 'unspeakable consolation' on finding a cave to hide in. These are touches of the tall story. That the 'stark naked' Friday should welcome the gift of clothes, or communicate elaborate information in sign language, is also unlikely. Fortunately most of the story is so credible that occasional implausibilities are not troublesome.

There are also some discrepancies. Crusoe's dates are often inconsistent, not only because he notches them up erratically; an amusing instance is his naming Friday from the day of his rescue, then later admitting that having lost 'an exact reckoning of days' he 'could never recover it again'. His Guinea voyage, we learn at one point, was his only successful one, yet the Brazil years leave him prosperous. In his first storm he prays fervently to God; cast on the island he thanks God in 'transports of the soul' and then compiles a balance-sheet of God's mercies; yet later, reviewing his past, he confesses that he 'never had once the word "Thank God" so much as on my mind, or in my mouth; nor in the greatest distress, had I so much as a thought to pray to Him'. He alternately has not and has English fellow-slaves at Sallee. On his first island night and during thirteen days salvage-gathering he does not mention rain, but his journal records rain all the first night and often thereafter (and the thirteen days become twenty-four). Sometimes he dreads mainland savages; sometimes he forgets them. The footprint terrifies him, yet the remains of the cannibal feast cause him 'no notions of danger'; then, religiously fortified, he feels much easier 'as to the safety of my circumstances', yet he remains 'pensive and sad ... within my own circle for almost two years'.

To harp on these points would be pedantic. Many seeming discrepancies can be explained: if on one page the wreck vanishes and on another it reappears, this may result from a tidal change; if Crusoe notches a pole to record time because he lacks writing materials, and later has such materials, this may result from another salvage trip; if sometimes he dreads and sometimes forgets mainland savages, this may be because he is obsessed about escaping; if he leaves Poll behind yet takes 'my parrot' with him, this may be another bird. This last (not very serious) suggestion shows how readily Defoe, if questioned, might head off objections.

After all, complete consistency of times, events, or opinions would be unnatural in 'reminiscences' supposedly recalled years afterwards. Touches of heightened colour and exaggeration are permissible in adventure stories: Crusoe is too alive, too human, to stick always to impeccable fact. And for one kind of exaggeration, the reformed hero's confessions of a 'wicked' past, a psychological explanation has already been suggested. Though he accuses himself, on no visible grounds, of being 'all that the most hardened, unthinking, wicked creature among our common sailors can be supposed to be', Crusoe never figures as other than a normal if imprudent man; his lurid view of his past owes something to the heightening common in popular fiction but mainly it is the standard self-abasement of the convert, a recrimination against himself which, misleading though it may be, often results from the new light in which the redeemed sinner sees bygone days. Nothing in his past, the convert thinks, can be accounted virtue in so black a soul.

Form and themes

Understandably, Defoe lacked the sense of controlled construction which later novelists have generally observed; *Robinson Crusoe*'s form is successive chance happenings, though a sense of evolution comes as his experience accumulates. It is nonetheless lifelike, indeed the more lifelike for this chanciness than many thoughtfully ordered narratives.

It is like anyone's life-story in two ways. First, things happen unpredictably yet credibly. Second, Crusoe like anyone else tries to trace some purpose in 'the course of my unaccountable life'. All may seem haphazard, progressing by galvanic impulses of the unexpected, whether from Crusoe's inner recklessness or from external chances; in his last pages he sums up his career as one of 'fortune and adventure, a life of

Providence's chequer-work'. Yet this acquires some sort of shape and significance as Crusoe moves from his initial inexperience and the uninteresting 'middle station' proposed for him, through successive ups and downs, to eventual if unstable success—'beginning foolishly, but closing much more happily than any part of [my life] ever gave me leave so much as to hope for'. His course develops, moreoever, in its crucial island stages, from poignant solitariness to social relations and companionship. Finally (and Defoe regarded this as a vital part of the book) it follows the pattern of spiritual autobiography, from neglect of God's plan, through wavering perceptions of his power, to a conviction of divine grace and favour. Thence arises a loose yet sturdy sense of form.

Such constructional themes, intermittent though they are, form Crusoe's story into some sort of whole, rather than the episodic jumble which is usual with adventure stories. All of us live, after all, through a succession of unpredictables, an enigmatic future of the unforeseen, yet in retrospect this may seem to assume shape as well as sequence. It is this instinctive sense of coherence which, perhaps accidentally rather than deliberately, Defoe's narrative expresses. Most of the story, moreover, occurs in one concentrated place (by contrast with his other biographies like *Moll Flanders, Captain Singleton, Colonel Jacque,* and *Roxana*), so Crusoe accumulates experience in an environment felt more and more as complete and comprehensible, where he can reflect on the perspective of his life. The island-frame holds the successive episodes in satisfyingly formal bounds.

Characterisation: Crusoe himself

From the preceding analysis the transition to Crusoe's character follows naturally: through him the book's whole bearing is conveyed. 'Human nature', Pope declared in the 408th *Spectator* (1712), 'is the most useful object of human reason, and to make the consideration of it pleasant and entertaining I always thought the best employment of human wit.' In this belief Pope's, and Defoe's, century concurred, and it is as a study of human nature that *Robinson Crusoe* has held its readers. As generic adventure story it has many rivals: as the life-story of one particular adventurer, in whom are concentrated so many human traits, hardly any.

Reason and impulse

Could Crusoe have read Pope's essay he would have found much to agree with, for, Pope says, 'the strange and absurd variety in men's actions shows plainly that they can never proceed immediately from reason. They must necessarily arise from the passions, which are to the mind as the winds to a ship. They only [the passions] can move it, and they too often destroy it'. This duality is the core of Crusoe's self-analysis.

Coming from settled industrious parents, he too should be settled and industrious. Sound education and social position point to that 'peace and plenty, ... temperance, moderation, quietness, health, society' which his father outlines; these benefits reward prudence and religious obedience.

Certainly Crusoe wants success. He is businesslike with associates, shrewd over affairs, and finally rewarded for his foresight. Energetic and dauntless, he solves problems, masters despondency ('I had learned not to despair of anything'), and labours for his salvation. Leslie Stephen, who judged the book one for boys, not men, because its 'amazing power of describing facts' far outdid any power in describing emotion, perversely thought Crusoe the non-romantic, no-nonsense 'beef-eating John Bull who has been shouldering his way through the world ever since'.

Yet already Crusoe's brothers have shown themselves rash, and he himself, 'possessed with a wandering spirit' (as *Farther Adventures* puts it), is impelled into his 'unaccountable life'. Why? This will now be examined.

The mysteries of motive

The first page hints at 'something fatal' in his disposition. This is felt sometimes as an external force ('my ill fate pushed me on'), sometimes as an internal one, but in effect these two are the same thing, some constituent implanted in him by 'fate', and 'impossible ... to escape', an 'impetuosity of desire' deaf to all reason. In his father's house it is 'the wild and undigested notion of raising my fortune'; in Brazil it is 'a rash and immoderate desire of rising'. Yet it takes other forms than mere economic ambition: it is an uncalculating, irrational urge.

Flouting obedience to God and to God's deputy his father, he commits his 'original sin', similar to that of Adam and Eve when in Eden they disobeyed God's command against tasting the fruit of good and evil. A deep sense of guilt follows, too matter-of-factly expressed perhaps to affect us deeply but still meant as real. To it we may apply what G. A. Starr remarks of Crusoe's whole religious bent: 'Surveys of his activities which take into account all that he builds and grows ... but omit or slight these religious observances are at best incomplete, and at worst seriously distorting.'

Crusoe's sense of guilt is psychologically true to human experience. But if retrospectively his early impulses seem 'wicked', his later ones seem 'secret intimations of Providence', 'invisible directions of God'. And in the last instalment of his story, *A Vision of the Angelic World*, which follows *Serious Reflections*, Crusoe observes, 'I know a man [Defoe, surely?] who made it his rule to obey these silent hints, and he has often declared to me that when he obeyed them he never miscarried, and if he neglected them ... he never succeeded'. Man, given reason by God, should obey it whenever it can elucidate his problems. But life depends largely on intuitions, and these, however unaccountable, will be bad guides to the faithless, good guides (God's voice) to the faithful.

Variations of mind and mood

Frequent public dispute had trained Defoe to weigh alternatives, and Crusoe perpetually carries on dialogues with his circumstances, indeed with his readers; he explains, speculates, evaluates. His story is more than a plain record; it speaks with a living voice. Will he obey, or disobey? will he follow wilful desire, or God's plan? will he choose this course or that in dilemma after dilemma? His brain is active; this is more evident in *Serious Reflections* and *A Vision of the Angelic World*, which discuss metaphysical matters, but it is apparent too in *Robinson Crusoe*, not only when Crusoe considers moral problems. He ranges over practical expedients, and broods about the lost Spanish sailors, chances of escape, island life generally (following the 'innumerable crowd of thoughts that whirled through that great thorow-fare of the brain'), dangers of savages, and the nature of cannibals.

His speculative range is paralleled by emotional range. 'Night and day' an obsession seizes him about killing cannibals; then he reflects he is unqualified to judge them, and feels almost fraternal towards them; yet when they re-appear he plunges again into a 'murdering humour'. The footprint swings him from religious confidence to long-lasting terror and for a time dispels his trust in God's protection. Such dramas of variable feeling are humanly credible; he is no rational stoic but a man of strong-minded moods.

Except for incidental extravagances such as have been mentioned Crusoe does not glamourise his story. His heroism is, as James Sutherland calls it, 'the heroism of the practical and the imperturbable [which] lives in an atmosphere ... of unemotional comment and habitual understatement'; yet his sobriety does not mean weak feeling, and Defoe could not have rendered his emotions so fully without a sense of identification: to quote Sutherland again, 'the frequent poignancy of feeling in *Robinson Crusoe*, and the intensity with which Defoe realises the loneliness and anguish of the hero, are compatible with some kind of self-involvement on the part of the author in the vicissitudes and sufferings he describes'. Crusoe, anyway, lives to feel as well as think and act. He records his father's grief touchingly and is affected by it, though transiently. His fears during the early storms are understandably intense, if melodramatically expressed. He is 'perfectly overwhelmed' when captured by the Turks, and feels 'inexpressible joy' on escaping. 'Ecstasies and transports of the soul' overcome him as he struggles ashore; the sprouting barley moves him to tears; the dream-vision stirs up 'horrors of [his] soul'. The ague casts him into torments of self-examination; the footprint appals him and a period ensues of morbid dread. In moods of religious trust he can be 'more happy in this forsaken, solitary condition than . . . in any other particular state in the world'; in other moods he feels his state 'the most miserable that could possibly be'. Such fluctuations are unsubtly managed; fictional psychology has not yet developed far, and Defoe more often states feelings than inwardly communicates them. Yet the 'frequent poignancy' of Sutherland's account is certainly there, and a sympathetic reading discovers much in Crusoe of emotional power.

He is not always agreeable. He deserts his home without a word of farewell or ever sending news; his family relationships on his return are bloodless; and his unfeeling disposal of Xury and the unworthy fears he harbours about Friday are displeasing. He goes his way essentially unattached despite yearning for companions when lonely, and despite valuing Friday's affection.

Yet this affection testifies to a humane if independent nature, and in other ways too he is likeable. The pleasure he takes in his pets, his pipe, and his comforts is appealing. He attracts honest and generous dealing from business associates, even when for years they hear nothing of him, and he treats them honourably too. In relaxed moments he shows a pleasant humour; with a 'merry reflection' he thinks of his royal state amidst 'subjects' all of whom hold different faiths yet enjoy 'liberty of conscience'; he sees the comedy of requiring written proofs of loyalty from castaways without pen and ink; and his account of Friday's bear-hunt is highly amusing.

That long solitude does not craze him, and that he adjusts so readily to life on and off the island, would, outside the book's covers, be hard to swallow. Yet within them he is so resourceful, so equipped by vitality of idea to master his circumstances, that he comes over impressively, and in his enterprising individualism he embodies the purposeful thrust of Defoe's age.

Characterisation: other characters

Of other characters little needs saying. Crusoe's father has no scope to be more than the 'wise and grave man' of his first appearance, the father-figure of the Prodigal-Son story who would welcome the wanderer back if given the chance. His significance is twofold: first, his fervent advice springs from patriarchal status, as the wise elder of tradition; second, he voices divine will, proclaiming the right way and the doom which attends the wrong. To this deep instinct Crusoe's insistence on original sin refers, and his father has a weight disproportionate to the few pages he occupies.

Then there are the associates who impinge on Crusoe in various ways—the courageous sailors and humane Yarmouth citizens; his first captain who warns him off the sea; the 'pretty good company' in London; his second 'honest and plain-dealing' captain who takes him to Guinea; that captain's excellent widow; his Portuguese rescuer; the Brazilian planters; the English merchants in Lisbon and London; and the administrators of his affairs. They are hardly individualised, yet collectively they contribute much. It is a reflection of Crusoe's nature that he finds honest people to deal with; it is also part of Defoe's nature to portray the world so uncynically. No one with worldly experience, admittedly, will trust naively; Crusoe hesitates before rescuing the shipwrecked Spaniards since men can prove ungrateful. Ships' crews, too, can be mutinous, and Crusoe deals firmly with the guilty. Yet true dealing is indeed commoner than false, otherwise society would collapse, and Crusoe's experience of general decency contributes a sturdy sense of rectitude which strengthens the book's appeal.

Finally there is Friday, who alone besides Crusoe earns extended attention. He adds a keen new interest: had Crusoe passed his island life companionless and then escaped unaided, much of human warmth would have been lost. Friday is advantageously displayed, handsome, 'very agreeable' in colour, attractive in expression, and exemplary in nature. Adaptable, he immediately abandons cannibalism, dons goatskin clothes, and soon complements a virtuoso command of explanatory gesture with serviceable English. He is so apt and cheerful that he reconciles Crusoe to island life. So 'faithful, loving, sincere' does he prove, 'without passions, sullenness, or designs', that Crusoe comes to realise that the non-Christian compares well with the Christian and indeed, if given the Christian's moral light, would do better by it than most Christians do.

Friday affects Crusoe as favourably as Crusoe does him. Crusoe can introduce him to novelties like clothes, tools, and guns (his initial awe of guns is charmingly described) and convert him to Christianity (while being somewhat patronising about his native religion—'poor ignorant creature', 'poor wild wretch', and so on). But debts are fully repaid, and Friday's merits need no patronising. His 'simple unfeigned honesty', intelligence, and passionate attachments (to Crusoe and his rescued father—quite movingly described) contribute richly to Crusoe's experience. Admitting that Friday becomes a better Christian than he is himself, Crusoe is fairmindedly generous about values to which Friday's admirable nature has led him.

Having made him so valuable on the island, Defoe seems lost as to what to do with him thereafter. After the lively but improbable Pyrenean episode he virtually drops him. When many writers, in Britain and elsewhere, were inventing foreign visitors who came and appraised Europe's manners and morals (commentaries by fictitious foreign observers were a favourite eighteenth-century literary device), Defoe utters not a word about Friday's long stay in England (supposedly 1687–1695), and barely mentions him in *Farther Adventures* until he makes Crusoe record with 'inexpressible grief' that he was killed in a skirmish with savages and buried at sea to an eleven-gun salute, 'the most grateful, faithful, honest, and most affectionate servant that ever man had'. The tribute is wholehearted, even if Friday has long been virtually absent; it truly reflects the esteem deserved by this simple good fellow who, never more than a servant, taught his master lessons in humanity.

Style and expression

Dampier, as has been mentioned, thought the right style for honest narrative should be unaffected and immediately intelligible, without art and pretension. This was a frequent theme in Defoe's time: the aim was to replace the elaborate rhetorics of the past with clear, natural language, in which the writer explained his meaning directly, and the reader was spared difficult syntax and vocabulary and any expectation that he should react with astonishment.

A century before *Robinson Crusoe*, Francis Bacon had proposed 'to set everything forth ... plainly and perspicuously': plainness of style ('nakedness' he called it) would show 'innocence and simplicity'. Bacon often ignored his own advice but others repeated his call. His secretary, Thomas Hobbes, who became the leading philosopher of the mid-seventeenth century, demanded 'perspicuous words ... by exact definitions purged from ambiguity', and argued that metaphors deceive like false lights. Bacon and Hobbes were pioneers of new modes of thought congenial to the developing natural sciences, and in a famous definition

Thomas Sprat, who in 1667 published a history of the young Royal Society (founded in 1662, and still Britain's main organ of scientific advance), told how the scientists rejected ornate style in favour of 'a close, naked, natural way of speaking; positive expressions; clear senses; a native easiness; . . . preferring the language of artisans, countrymen, and merchants before that of wits or scholars'.

Not scientists alone but religious and political thinkers sought clear, natural utterance, in fields where heady polemics in highwrought rhetoric had long inflamed passions and perplexed ideas. A prominent seventeenth-century churchman, Samuel Parker, even wanted laws against 'fulsome and luscious metaphors' to cure 'all our present distempers': make men 'speak sense as well as truth' without 'fine metaphors and glittering allusions', he declared, and fanatical extravagance would appear 'empty nonsense'. His advice still holds good.

This was indeed a real need. The ideal sought throughout dispute-torn Europe was, as one of Defoe's poetic contemporaries wrote, a style attainable 'When through the phrase we plainly see the sense'; and what Pope's *Essay on Criticism* (1711—the age's critical creed) wants from intellect is 'Something whose truth convinced at sight we find'. True style lucidly expresses true meanings. This is the clear, social way to write, so that (to quote Goldsmith's praise of an exemplary stylist) the reader 'wonders why he himself did not think or speak in that very manner'. Swift, whose idea of good style was 'proper words in proper places', described it as working by direct transference of distinct thought: 'when a man's thoughts are clear, the properest words will generally offer themselves first; and his own judgement will direct him in what order to place them, so as they may best be understood' (*Letter to a Young Gentleman Lately Entered into Holy Orders*, 1720).

Defoe's idiom is that of the practical citizen rather than the man of letters, so it is even closer to the 'close, naked, natural way'. In *The Complete English Tradesman* he expressed his ideal: 'Easy, plain, and familiar language is the beauty of speech in general, and is the excellency of all writing, on whatever subject, or to whatever persons they are we write or speak. That way of speaking which is most easily understood is the best way of speaking.' And in *Serious Reflections* he confirmed the equation of plain, honest style and plain, honest dealing: 'The plainness I profess, both in style and method, seems to have some suitable analogy to the subject, honesty. . . . The plainness of expression . . . will give no disadvantage to my subject, since honesty shows the more beautiful . . . when artifice is dismissed.' His plainness and honesty are those of the educated, vigorous, straight-speaking man of the people; his truth is no poetic impression or fine-spun speciality but the firm facts for which the words are the unambiguous equivalent. From the first sentence to the end, this cogent, natural voice speaks forth.

It is the educated speech of ordinary folk, unconcerned with polish, musicality, or poetic charm, aiming neither at high and cultivated tastes nor at low and crude ones, the natural address of such a practical yet intelligent man as Crusoe, and it looks for popular acceptance (taking that term to mean not any debased or trivialised gratification but an enquiring interest in genuine experience). It accords with Locke's pronouncement that God has 'designed man as a sociable creature [and] furnished him with language ... to be the common tie of society' (*Essay Concerning Human Understanding* (1690), III. 1. i).

The tone is companionable, attentive to the reader's convenience, and, because it expresses convincing facts, evidently trustworthy. The manner is helpfully informative, and each phrase sounds with down-to-earth assurance. The words are ordinary, uncoloured, courteous, like sensible talk. The sentences, though, have more form than those of spontaneous conversation; this is a written, purposeful style, not a tape-recorded transcript. Defoe (trained for the ministry and skilled in controversy) and Crusoe (a man of education and orderly ideas) ally the direct energies of speech with the effective structures that eighteenth-century literary disciplines made natural.

If we begin the examination of Defoe's style negatively, by saying that it lacks many resources of verbal enrichment—resources such as simile, metaphor, irony, rhythmical artifice, scene-elaboration, atmospheric suggestion, rhetorical figures, verbal texture, and the like—this is to point to its positives. It spurns these to work more directly. No sophistications are to share the reader's attention to the matter in hand.

One resource it does employ plentifully—imagery. The book abounds in things; this is a major effect. Defoe's world is full of the physical objects of practical life, and excitement spreads from the page as they are enumerated, the abounding real implements and materials with which man must deal. But this is imagery in the elementary sense, things described merely as their existence or behaviour affects Crusoe's situation. If they have any symbolic overtone it is only the simplest, that man must deal with his world and that that world is one in which the primary qualities of mass and motion mean far more than any secondary sensuous or aesthetic appeals.

Crusoe often invites us into the story by his free-flowing conversational manner—in the family history, for instance, or through the African voyage, or by surveys of island life with its arrangements and achievements. Where no dramatic tension or emotion arises the tone is easy, the sentences spontaneously evolving (it seems) with clauses loosely attached but in their pith and point proving that Crusoe has a shrewd command of his meaning. In such readily-running sentences items flow one from another just as he chooses to furnish us with them. Perhaps 'chooses' sounds too deliberate: they seem the unselected awarenesses of his mind. Yet 'selected' is just what they are, selected skilfully to seem unselected, to give the right mixture of fact, information, reaction, and onward movement which carries us naturally along. The account of the storm off Yarmouth can be taken as representative. It really seems to enact the sequence of true events; the prose is as it were on-the-spot recording, its form dictated not by artistic deliberation but by what actually happened. In this there is admirable art—it does not happen mindlessly—but the art is that of seeming unartful.

True to stylistic naturalism the prose is studded with colloquial idiom, sometimes slightly archaic, expressing that 'general vulgar [=common] sense' of language which Defoe demanded. Here it lacks the pungency of the market-place which in controversial writings Defoe excelled in; Crusoe's nature and purpose dictate good manners. But there is a satisfying speech flavour of ordinary folk, if a little old-fashioned. Crusoe is always heard as a person, telling of direct experience. (How effective this is is evident if we turn to *Farther Adventures*, where for a long space most of the vivacity goes while Crusoe tells the secondhand story of island events during his absence.) He tosses in personal ejaculations—'I say', 'I assure you', 'I must confess', 'God knows', 'you may be sure', 'you are to understand', 'it might be so for all I know', 'Who would ha' supposed we were sailed on to the southward . . . ?' and the like. Popular idiom is frequent enough to freshen the prose without vulgarising it—'expecting every moment when the ship would go to the bottom', 'your father's words are fulfilled upon you', 'our master will not be thus served', 'he swam so strong' (=strongly), 'we slept none' (=not at all), 'I run forward' (=ran), 'it was a terrible great lion', 'he found he was gotten on the west of Guinea', 'it wanted but a little that my cargo had slipped off', Friday's bear 'shuffling along at a strange rate', and so on. This is popular, not polished, speech.

Its companionable tone accords with the pleasant humour which (like Goldsmith's affability later) relates things clearly and appreciatively. A good instance is Crusoe's meeting with the wild cat, just after his second visit to the wreck. Another is the account of his pastoral realm with his herds of goats and the agreeable pets. This is warm with pleasant yet alert ease. He jokes about his formidable moustaches, or his 'wooden' (clumsy) handling of his wooden spade. Later, the story of Friday's bear-hunt is sharply entertaining with its keenly observed comic action. At moments, too, the style achieves a limpid and grateful clarity of tenderness, even of charm: Crusoe's return to his 'old hutch' after his island exploration, and his fostering his captive kid, sound with true sentiment, as too does his description of the rescued Friday.

But familiarity and pleasantness do not mean slackness. If the style sometimes relaxes, even rambles, it is never flabby; its meanderings are always relevant, however casual they seem. And predominantly, as has been said, it is braced by its age's sense of discipline. It can strongly and sharply record the successive moments of dramatic events, stroke by firm stroke, so that even in a quick-moving scene the constituents are clear and unconfused; the whole story of Friday's escape is a model of its kind, and there are many comparable examples. Time and again sentences move with unforced assurance, and the crispest sense of phrasal timing, to an incisive point. Examples could be innumerable, but two must suffice, the accounts of Crusoe's departure from home, and of his consternation at the footprint. Here they are (pages 31, 162):

> (*a*) I consulted neither father or mother any more, nor so much as sent them word of it; but leaving them to hear of it as they might, without asking God's blessing, or my father's, without any consideration of circumstances or consequences, and in an ill hour, God knows, on the first of September 1651 I went on board a ship bound for London.
>
> (*b*) I stood like one thunder-struck, or as if I had seen an apparition; I listened, I looked round me, I could hear nothing, nor see anything; I went up to a rising ground to look farther; I went up the shore and down the shore, but it was all one, I could see no other impression but that one. I went to it again to see if there were any more, and to observe if it might not be my fancy; but there was no room for that, for there was exactly the very print of a foot, toes, heel, and every part of a foot; how it came thither I knew not, nor could in the least imagine.

Pith, economy, and punchy rhythm join; each phrase clips into place, not because any artificial form is predetermined for it but because essential points are to be made—ticked off, as it were—without fluff or fuss, to define the position. It is a style, too, which sharpens readily into aphorism—'All our discontents about what we want appeared to me to spring from the want of thankfulness for what we have', or, 'I wanted nothing but what I had, and had nothing but what I wanted'. There is a healthy definitiveness about it.

Because of this sinewy skill in definition it is good at dramatic timing.

As one of many instances take the moment when Crusoe dislodges his Moorish boatmate during the escape from Sallee; this moves by brisk stages to the point where 'I took him by surprise with my arm under his twist [=crotch], and tossed him clean overboard into the sea'. The action moves exactly as the real thing would have done, and this is the point of Defoe's athletic directness throughout—it sharpens everything for our alerted attention.

But Defoe manages more than readably vivid narration sharpened with vivid vignettes. He can deal with large events dramatically, even intensely. The storm which drives Crusoe ashore on the island is told with masterly power; the force of narration is that not of sensationalism or melodrama but of accurate and convincing reality. There are few of the usual means of scene-painting—emotion-raising verbs, colourful adjectives and adverbs, sound effects, and the like; all is done through capturing the helpless actions of the crew and the force of wind and wave by plain statement of fact. Plain though it may be, it gives all the evidence needed for grasping the scene, and the paragraphs in which Crusoe is swept by the waves on to the shore are superbly strenuous. Defoe ignores the fact, and the reader cares nothing for it, that Crusoe supposedly is writing thirty years and thousands of miles away and would hardly recapture so vividly the overwhelming confusion of shipwreck. What tells is the immediate conviction of truth; it really was just as Crusoe relates it, of this we feel sure. We go through it with him, in the very present moment. Such imaginative truth of realisation is magnificent. Its truth of insight is such that Crusoe is, as he would in fact be, so physically involved in the struggle for breath, so wholly absorbed in physical sensation, as to have virtually no time for emotional reaction until, cast on shore, he can realise in transports of relief all he has been through.

The later occasion when he is swept by the current out to the limitless sea is told with less dynamic power but much more psychological tension: he has time to realise his peril, and the narrative is a fine blend of fact and feeling, told still with that fidelity which seems to give the unvarnished reality of things. The point may be made again; this is a story identified with its narrator, a narrator who records the external world with objective truth yet responds to it as personal experience. The experience is, however, related not as evidence to show how remarkable a fellow he is but as what anyone else would feel in his place. Never was 'autobiography' less egotistic.

That is the style's essence, a man speaking to men, predominantly in plain monosyllabic words and the commonest parts of speech; its vocabulary is firm and concrete. Robert Frost the American poet said of his own writing that he aimed at being as natural as a potato, but a potato clean of soil: Defoe's is the same.

Yet it is not without passion. Crusoe's self-reproaches, religious reflections, and passages of yearning, hope, and dread are eloquent, and Friday's reunion with his father is related fervently yet without sentimental indulgence. Defoe's 'artless' style proves, in fact, to have many resources; it can be factually businesslike, familiar and free-running, pithy and pointed, realistically powerful, and emotionally charged. At different times it is quick and brisk, leisurely and easy, urgent and tense, strong and impressive.

It rises when necessary to those ordered forms which the eighteenth century found natural, arranging things for the mind to grasp methodically. Crusoe describes his island resources thus (pages 139–140):

> I had no competitor, none to dispute sovereignty or command with me. I might have raised ship loadings of corn; but I had no use for it; so I let as little grow as I thought enough for my occasion. I had tortoise or turtles enough; but now and then one was as much as I could put to any use. I had timber enough to have built a fleet of ships. I had grapes enough to have made wine, or to have cured into raisins, to have loaded that fleet when they had been built. But all I could make use of was all that was valuable. I had enough to eat and to supply my wants, and what was all the rest to me? If I killed more flesh than I could eat, the dog must eat it, or the vermin. If I sowed more corn than I could eat, it must be spoiled. The trees that I cut down were lying to rot on the ground. I could make no more use of them than for fuel; and that I had no occasion for, but to dress my food.

Everything falls unobtrusively into place, in a scheme so unforced that we never feel it is artificial, yet it presents things in simple definitive patterns for the mind's immediate grasp.

The sentences here are short and firm, but they can also be long without losing direction. When at the beginning Crusoe's father exhorts him he does so in unusually protracted sentences (two exceed 250 words each); nevertheless they are so orderly, clause by parallel clause, that his whole meaning forms itself unstrained, and indeed through successive waves of idea expresses a most impressive weight of earnestness. In many of Crusoe's reflective analyses his whole train of thought is organised in long (but not over-formal) sentence patterns which clearly arrange his meaning for us. This happens when, for example, terrified by the footprint, Crusoe examines the instability of human feelings (in the paragraph starting 'How strange a chequer-work of Providence is the life of man!'), or when, having decided he should not slaughter the cannibals no matter how horrid their practices, he reflects on the 'merciful disposition of Heaven', or, valuing Friday's virtues, wonders why God should withhold true faith from so many of mankind, or feels comfort in Friday's conversion.

Defoe's style, then, may look informal, even casual, but whether in practical business, or reflective analysis, or passionate outbreak, it effectively gives the reader what he needs.

An age of enterprise

Two aspects remain for consideration concerning the economic and religious nature of Defoe's time: a brief discussion may set the book against the background of national life. *Robinson Crusoe* is not, as some commentators suggest, an economic parable, but it stirs the blood with the excitements of travel, trade, profit and loss, and the practicalities of labour.

A medal struck in 1670 may serve as a symbol: it shows the world marked out in latitude and longitude and it is inscribed *Diffusus in Orbe Britannus*—the Briton spread throughout the world. Since the sixteenth century England had experienced widespread economic development, reflected in the founding of London's Royal Exchange (the centre of mercantile activity) and great trading companies with agencies far overseas. Banks and insurance companies followed by the early eighteenth century. Projects multiplied at home and abroad, for land reclamation, better communications, agricultural improvement, mechanical inventions, improved chronometers and other navigational aids, exploration and foreign settlement: before 1700 England's only colonies were Jamaica, and the thirteen on the American seaboard; by 1713 others had been added in the Mediterranean, West Indies, and Canada, and thereafter acquisitions multiplied.

Robinson Crusoe is the most remarkable of many works inspired by overseas enterprise, but excitement at new horizons was widespread. The best writer of light verse in Defoe's time, Matthew Prior, celebrated the theme in his *Carmen Seculare for the Year 1700*:

> *Through various climes, and to each distant pole,*
> *In happy tide let active commerce roll;*
> *Let Britain's ships export our annual fleece*
> *Richer than Argo brought to ancient Greece;*
> *Returning loaded with the shining stores*
> *Which lie profuse on either India's shores*

(the shores, that is, of East and West Indies). 'The commerce of England', Defoe himself observed in *A Plan of the English Commerce* (1728), 'is an immense and almost incredible thing.' At the outset of Sir Robert Walpole's long prime ministership (1721–1742) his programme was announced to Parliament as follows: 'We should be extremely wanting to ourselves if we neglected to improve the favourable opportunity ... of extending our commerce, upon which the riches and grandeur of this nation chiefly depend'; and Walpole's tenure of office was marked by the pre-eminence given to economic growth. In a tribute to him the poet Richard Savage extolled the spirit of home and foreign enterprise:

> *Abroad the merchant, while the tempests rave,*
> *Adventurous sails, nor fears the wind and wave;*
> *At home untired we find the auspicious hand [i.e. of Liberty]*
> *With flocks and herds and harvests bless the land ...*
> *Thus stately cities, statelier navies rise,*
> *And spread our grandeur under distant skies.*

In similar spirit Savage prefaced his verses *Of Public Spirit in Regard to Public Works* (*c*.1730) with a prospectus:

> Of reservoirs and their uses; of draining fens, and building bridges, cutting canals, repairing harbours and stopping inundations, making rivers navigable, building light-houses: of agriculture, gardening, and planting for the noblest uses: of commerce: of public roads: of public buildings, viz. squares, streets, mansions, palaces, courts of justice, senate-houses, theatres, hospitals, churches, colleges.

National life, certainly, has always required business, but for complex historical reasons Defoe's age felt unprecedented excitement about it. Dissenters like him, debarred from English universities and the professions, entered with particular energy into trade and industry, and shrewd enterprise became the leading tenet of their lives. But not Dissenters only: this was a general trend. What Defoe called 'the grand affair of business' inspired an outburst of initiatives. In the 21st *Spectator* (1711) Addison praised trade which lets all men of foresight exert their talents. John Locke, the age's ruling philosopher, urged his compatriots to be 'well-skilled in knowledge of material causes and effects ... [with] improvement of such arts and inventions, engines and utensils, as might best contribute to ... conveniency and delight'. Robert Boyle, an eminent philosopher-scientist and early member of the Royal Society, declared that the Society valued only knowledge with 'a tendency to use'. Nothing could better describe Defoe's own leanings. At his death his library's sale catalogue offered 'several hundred Curious, Scarce Tracts on ... Husbandry, Trade, Voyages, Natural History, Mines, Minerals, &c.', and one of his *Review* papers (21 June 1711) is an allegory about Invention, son of Necessity and Poverty, who devises 'improvements of land, art [=practical skills], and various contrivances for ... advantage'. Descended from Invention is Trade, originating 'the virtues and uses of many unknown things, the value of jewels, the price and use of money, shipping, and all the improvements of navigation'. And in a famous cartoon sequence, *Industry and Idleness* (1747), the artist William Hogarth depicted the industrious apprentice prospering through honest work, marrying his master's daughter, and becoming Lord Mayor of London, while his wastrel fellow sinks through crime to the gallows. This parable any right-minded citizen would applaud.

Wars were waged for commercial rather than religious or dynastic reasons, and the treaties which ended them included commercial clauses. Parliament promoted laws for encouraging trade, improving land-usage, and constructing roads and canals. The results were less radical than those of the 'Industrial Revolution' after the mid-eighteenth century, for most Britons still lived by old habits, but they were notable enough, and Defoe expressed the ambitions which prompted them when in *Farther Adventures* he had Crusoe meet an English merchant in Bengal. 'The whole world is in motion, rolling round and round', the merchant observes, 'all the creatures of God, heavenly bodies and earthly, are busy and diligent; why should we be idle?' At home, in the *Tour thro' ... Great Britain*, Defoe voiced the national urge for construction: 'The new buildings erected, the old buildings taken down; new discoveries in metals, mines, minerals; new undertakings in trade; inventions, engines, manufactures in a nation pushing and improving as we are; these things open new scenes every day, and make England especially show a new and differing face in many places, on every occasion of surveying it.' The spirit is one we now associate rather with modern America or progressive parts of the developing world.

The status of the merchant, industrialist, or projector rose, by comparison with that of the traditional gentry. But if progressive 'new men' like the significantly-named Sir Andrew Freeport of *The Spectator*, No. 2 (1711), 'a merchant of great eminence ... noble and generous ... acquainted with commerce in all its parts', or Mr Sealand of Steele's comedy *The Conscious Lovers* (1723) seemed alien to conservative landowners, much was written to prove their interests harmonious. The 76th *Guardian* (1713) assures landowners that the prosperity which foreign trade creates will enrich agriculture at home.

Sir Andrew Freeport and his country friend Sir Roger de Coverley get on amiably together, and Sir Andrew himself at last retires to a rural estate determined 'to make it as beautiful a spot as any in her majesty's dominions' (*Spectator*, 1712, No. 549). In like spirit Crusoe himself, seafarer, trader, and colonist, returns from his island, buys a country farm in *Farther Adventures*, and starts 'cultivating, managing, planting, and improving', believing this (until his urge for travel re-asserts itself) 'the most agreeable life that Nature was capable of directing'. A zest for 'improving' fired energetic minds in town and country alike to homebred or overseas projects.

The keys to success were steadiness, not rashness; integrity, not trickery; industry, not negligence; practical, not extravagant, aims. Given 'regular and orderly disposition', *The Spectator* proclaimed (No. 283), men of normal gifts prosper; without it, 'the greatest parts and most lively imaginations' perish. The 'middle state' recommended by Crusoe's father, the methodical prosperity Crusoe attains in Brazil—these are the due expectations of men steady in their callings. This, in a way, was a modern-materialist version of the old classical maxim of the 'Golden Mean', the even course of life neither too high nor too low, which a minor poet, Henry Baker (Defoe's son-in-law), desired in his *Original Poems* (1725)—'Give me, you Gods, before I die/An happy mediocrity'. It also claimed religious endorsement as God's plan for the obedient: an eminent bishop, Benjamin Hoadly, praised the middle state in the fifteenth of his *Twenty Sermons* (1756) since 'it doth not, by its natural tendency, so much endanger virtue as either of the two extremes, of riches or poverty'.

All these considerations focus on Crusoe. Born of creditably successful parents, a man of the world, energetic, ardent for success, practical, materially minded, honest though hard-headed, given generally to rational assessments of the main chance, he should be the ideal subject for that 'calling' of perseverance towards attainable ambitions which his father urges on him. He can observe practical processes, master difficulties, control others, and work with partners. He seems the very personification of his age's ideal, and he has indeed been repeatedly held up as the spirit of Economic Man, of his own time and others.

Yet there is a great qualification. Economic Man is more than the steady calculator sitting in an office and going about the safer routines of business. Crusoe's 'projects and undertakings beyond my reach' and 'rash and immoderate desire of rising faster than the nature of the thing admitted' are part of Economic Man too. He adventures, as well as accumulates. When Crusoe sees his own extravagances as disobedience to God's and his father's wills he is viewing things conventionally. But if God warrants material success, he warrants risk-taking as well as playing safe. Crusoe of course considers his impulses to be against God (even, by implication, to be inspired by the Devil). But Economic Man is as likely to dare and to be imaginative as to stick to any 'middle state', and if 'the whole world ... heavenly bodies and earthly' is 'in motion, rolling round and round' is not this by divine dynamics? Crusoe in fact embodies his age in both its steady practicality and its adventurousness. To take the former alone to be God's plan is to heed steady-middle-class orthodoxy. But to crush adventurous impulse is to deny a fundamental urge, doubtless also part of the divine scheme and of Economic Man too. Crusoe in fact ends prosperously: what he early feels as sinful selfwill changes, as he becomes religious, into a sense of inward providential guidance. Caution and risk, steadiness and impulse, order and freedom are twin sides of life.

This is not a Marxist analysis: it follows no economic theory but what happens in the book. Yet a Marxist writer, Christopher Caudwell, has most challengingly put this aspect of the 'bourgeois', the middle-class man of business, who, in Caudwell's words, 'sees himself as a heroic figure fighting a lone fight for freedom, as the individualist battling against all the social relations which fetter the natural man'. The 'bourgeois' writer, likewise, reflects this species, the imaginative man eager for autonomy, who 'sees himself as an individualist striving to realise what is most essentially himself by an expansive outward movement of the energy of his heart, by a release of internal force which outward forms are crippling'. Among the representatives of this ethos Caudwell offers Crusoe.

Since an 'expansive outward movement of the energy of his heart' galvanises Economic Man, as it does Defoe and Crusoe, it exerts itself in overseas trade. For a century, corporations like the East India and Levant companies had extended exotic traffic and imaginative horizons. Great explorations mapped the world and brought home its mysteries. Fascinating products flowed to and from Europe, east and west, south and north. Thomas Tickell, a minor literary man, wrote, *Lines on the Prospect of Peace* (1713), expressing the expansive zest of the time:

> *Fearless our merchant now pursues his gain,*
> *And roams securely o'er the boundless main;*
> *Now o'er his head the polar Bear he spies,*
> *And freezing spangles of the Lapland skies;*
> *Now swells his canvas to the sultry Line [i.e. Equator]*
> *With glitt'ring spoils where Indian grottoes shine,*
> *Where fumes of incense glad the southern seas,*
> *And wafted citron scents the balmy breeze.*

Addison's Royal-Exchange *Spectator* (No. 69) portrays a colourful cosmopolitan company of the world's merchants trafficking in their commodities, and it rejoices that 'our rooms are filled with pyramids of China, and adorned with the workmanship of Japan. Our morning's draught comes to us from the remotest corners of the earth. We repair our bodies by the drugs of America, and repose ourselves under Indian canopies'. Poets, as we have seen, sounded the same note: Pope's society belle in *The Rape of the Lock* gathers the world's luxuries on her dressing table. Over all such activities Defoe's mind zestfully hovered. When at the end of *Farther Adventures* Crusoe returns to England, he has crossed Asia by camel-caravan freighted with silk, calicoes, tea, and spices; Defoe's Captain Singleton takes a cargo of cloth to the East Indies and then sails piratically about the Indian Ocean, seeking Spanish treasure-ships, East-India merchantmen, and Chinese trading junks. Most foreign voyaging, though, was lawful, and meant, in the words of James Thomson's poem *Liberty* (1736),

Instead of treasure robb'd by ruffian war,
Round social earth to circle fair exchange,
And bind the nations in a golden chain.

Such were the stimuli of foreign trade.

Robinson Crusoe, then, richly represents its time, not through any sophisticated plan on Defoe's part but because his was a mind charged with contemporary interests, those concerning sheer utility, and those others concerning risky ventures prompted equally by hopes of profit and the thirst for excitement. Crusoe is caught between 'middle state' stability and the heart's 'expansive outward movement', between sober practicality and romantic risk. All these ran deep in the age.

Religious bearings

The scattered comments hitherto devoted to the book's religious bearings now need gathering together, however briefly. Earth and heaven, it was commonly held, both reward honest industry: 'you may gain enough of both worlds if you would mind each in its place', as one moralist put it. *Robinson Crusoe* reflects this assumption as it reflects economic ideas too. Not everyone is impressed however; 'were anyone's religious emotions ever aroused either by Crusoe's story or his meditations?' a recent critic has asked. Yet Defoe's age might be more respectful: Crusoe's religious evolution, John Richetti comments in *Popular Fiction Before Richardson* (1969), 'is in the context of the age a heroic and controversial act'; he is a religious explorer as well as intrepid traveller and courageous castaway.

Is it naive to think so? His evolution is intermittent, and soberly rather than intensely treated, yet the cumulative effect is considerable. Crusoe's faith, writes James Sutherland, 'like everything else about him on the island, ... is homemade and not of the finest quality. [But] it is sound, and it will stand up to daily use'. And it counts for much in the story.

Crusoe develops from the selfwilled unenlightened state representing 'the general plague of mankind', and from acting 'like a mere brute from the principles of nature and by the dictates of common sense only'—that is, by heedless impulse and worldly inclination. The stirrings of his spirit, climaxed during his self-examination while ague-struck and miserable, convince him of his insufficiency. This is the first of two crucial steps. This step is negative, the negating of selfwill by humility. The second is positive, an overpowering sense that God fathoms the soul. Crusoe's pilgrimage wavers; good fortune will turn him to God, a scare like the footprint will dispel his 'due temper for application to my Maker'. Helped by Bible texts he must advance by experience, reflection, and analysis from the state where 'the word had no sound', through the recognition of his errors, to the first deep prayers which prompt the 'hope that God would hear', and the realisation that spiritual salvation far outweighs physical. Thence follow religious trust and acceptance, reverence, a daily 'sense of God's goodness' and, when Friday is converted, 'a secret joy' throughout his soul. All this culminates, as he prepares to embark, in a passion of religious gratitude.

The process is one of firsthand experience guided by the Bible and simple faith, the belief that God relates personally to his creatures. Except for some late, brief, though fervent, mention of Jesus Christ as the key to eternal life, and to the Devil as the evil power (Friday's queries about this prove sorely embarrassing), Crusoe barely acknowledges theological dogma. Faith's requirements, he holds, are 'plainly laid down' in the Bible, and those disputes which have lacerated Christendom are worse than useless.

Robinson Crusoe is in fact closer to *Serious Reflections* than is sometimes recognised: its own serious reflections count for much. The moral earnestness and quiet reverence with which Defoe's age was replacing previous centuries' doctrinal violence are part of its central meaning; the 'heroic and controversial act' of Crusoe's progress partakes of a broad contemporary move towards soul-searching and away from doctrinaire rigour, a moral evolution which sought humble honesty within oneself and charity towards others. Crusoe will help others towards his own beliefs, but if they have other convictions he respects their consciences.

Part 4
Hints for study

Key points for attention

Robinson Crusoe is easy to read but not entirely easy to study. Its episodes are clear, but the narrative is informal, and Crusoe's character, though credible, fluctuates with changing predicaments and moods. In these ways it resembles the haphazard processes of nature rather than the disciplines of art. Defoe professes merely to be an editor, not the master of the narrative as, later, Fielding would be in *Tom Jones* (1749) or Thackeray in *Vanity Fair* (1848). For study, one would welcome a firmer shape than the story offers.

The book's main elements are its adventures, and the man who incurs them. The readiest way to grasp it is to concentrate on the most striking of the former, and the main qualities of the latter. In between, there will be bridging passages of lesser force; Crusoe's quieter phases make pleasant reading and indicate that island experience can be agreeably relaxed as well as testingly strenuous, but it suffices to recall them as the setting to the stronger episodes which form good short stories in themselves.

Selecting some major events, you should ask how each makes its impact: by quiet start working to powerful climax? by powerful start with disturbing sequel (like the earthquake-and-storm, or the footprint)? by physical-practical interest (like the salvage scenes, or pottery making)? by tense excitement (like Friday's rescue)? by strong subjective agitation (like the ague-fit and dream-vision)? by bodily turbulence (like the wreck and near-drowning)? The range of such events suggests something of Defoe's creative power. Do you agree that, telling stories apparently artlessly, Defoe chooses his means effectively and qualifies as a 'great artist'?

Similarly with Crusoe's character: what are its main traits? his practical skill? dynamic energies? self-possession? impulsiveness? variety of moods? individualism? relations with others? adaptability (himself to the island and vice versa)? acceptance or repining at solitude? growth of reflection and analysis? Is he a figurehead or a convincing human being? What values does he live by?

Then, in its main bearings, what constitutes the book's wide appeal?

If, as has been said, '*Robinson Crusoe* is far from being merely a novel of romantic adventure', what more is it? Is Crusoe somehow universal, reflecting a general human condition, some thirst in the human imagination? Given that many eighteenth-century writers aimed at a restricted, cultured, audience, and Defoe at a large unspecialised one, what strengths of writing did this encourage? Any weaknesses?

Significant passages

(*Page references are to the Penguin English Library edition.*)
(*i*) Paternal exhortations (27-29); (*ii*) the storms off Yarmouth (33-36) and in the Atlantic (63); (*iii*) sense of 'ill fate' (37); (*iv*) Portuguese captain's kindness (54-55); (*v*) 'the dictates of my fancy' (60; and similar themes elsewhere); (*vi*) danger of drowning (64-65); (*vii*) sprouting barley (94-95); (*viii*) earthquake and storm (96-97); (*ix*) dream-vision and self-examination (102-111); (*x*) pottery-making (131-133); (*xi*) assessment after the fourth year (139-144); (*xii*) garments and appearance (144-146,158-159); (*xiii*) the footprint (162-168); (*xiv*) thoughts about cannibals (175-179); (*xv*) pets (185-186); (*xvi*) Spanish wreck (191-198); (*xvii*) Friday's escape (204-209); (*xviii*) Friday's conversion (218-223); (*xix*) rescues of the Spanish captain and Friday's father (231-241); (*xx*) rescue of the English captain and defeat of the mutineers (248-269); (*xxi*) return to England (274-275, 298); (*xxii*) Brazilian prosperity (275-283); (*xxiii*) Friday and the bear (287-290).

Arranging material for answers

Three main stages are involved: first, settling what the question means; second, gathering evidence; third, arranging the argument persuasively.

(i) The meaning of the question

A question asks you to demonstrate something. It may require straightforward illustration or, perhaps, decision between differing views.

If, for instance, it asks you to illustrate how Defoe manages realistic effects, then after briefly explaining what these are (effects resembling the practical particulars or normal sensations of real life, without being subtle or sophisticated—even though some real life occurrences are so), the answer will show that Defoe does make his story look authentic; he convinces us that the story records such facts and feelings as we should experience were we present, however romantic the adventures may be.

If elements in the story strike you as unconvincing, then mentioning them would usefully supplement your argument about the realism of

Hints for study · 69

the rest; this should be kept brief, but it would show your thoughtful assessment.

The question, then, is answered when you produce evidence demonstrating what is asked for.

A question may, however, invite arguments. If, instead of asking how Defoe makes *Robinson Crusoe* look realistic, it asks you to discuss 'Defoe was simply a narrator of plain facts' and you disagree, the answer should have two main areas. One would show that he is indeed such a narrator: the other would, probably, argue that he was more than 'simply' this. But if you agreed with the proposition, the two areas would be reversed; first you would recognise that many readers have thought him more than 'simply' this (because he includes thoughts, feelings, and significances beyond plain facts); then you would argue that, nevertheless, the plain facts are what give the book its hold.

The question, again, might be the converse of that about plain facts, and assert that 'It is imagination that counts in *Robinson Crusoe*'. The answer should still fall into two areas: one area would recognise that much in it looks unimaginative; the other would argue that, nevertheless, qualities like the selection of detail, dramatic emphases, and sympathetic insights into Crusoe show imagination, and that these creative elements raise the book above a prosaic record. Alternatively, if you disagreed with the assertion, you might begin by recognising that imaginative qualities have often been claimed for it, but then argue that what seizes readers is the sheer photographic lifelikeness of the contents, which may strike us as less imaginative than merely reproductive. If, for instance, one knows how to make pots and writes the process down, would the account, however interesting, differ materially from Crusoe's description? (The answer is probably 'yes'; but to show why is critically interesting.)

(ii) Gathering evidence

You must, of course, survey the evidence before deciding how to answer. From the book, or your notes, you will gather material to present your case. In answering, do not copy long passages of text, though apt short phrases will sharpen your argument and show you have read alertly. Reference to specific details or procedures is better than long quotation: if, say, you discuss Crusoe's struggles while being swept ashore, a transcription of Defoe's account does no good: what does good is your own comments on the waves' force, the beatings back and forward, the effort and choking, the struggle with the undertow, the impact with the rocks, and so on.

(iii) Arranging the argument

In arranging your argument, briefly recognise what if anything might be said against the case you are to put. Then say why you think differently; put first the lightest items, then the medium ones, then the weightiest, to provide a climax. This gives a movement forwards and upwards, and leaves a firm conclusion in the mind.

Specimen questions

(*i*) 'If ever the story of any private man's adventures in the world were worth making public, ... the editor of this account thinks this will be so' (*Robinson Crusoe*, Preface). What points would you offer to justify this assumption?

(*ii*) 'By sympathy and insight, Defoe creates living characters.' Discuss and illustrate.

(*iii*) How does a book centred upon a single character create such variety of interest?

(*iv*) Examine Crusoe as a man torn between reason which tells him to 'follow his calling' and 'triumphant passions which force him to wander'.

(*v*) 'Defoe succeeds in the short episode: for long narrative he lacks controlling form.' How far do you agree? Illustrate your answer.

(*vi*) 'Realism pursued through the imagination'—how far do you find this in *Robinson Crusoe*?

(*vii*) 'Defoe so masks his art that we may not realise how he manages his narrative.' Discuss, illustrating your answer from two or three areas of the story.

(*viii*) How do the style and handling of *Robinson Crusoe* create its air of authenticity?

Model answers

QUESTION: **How impressive do you find the moral and religious elements in *Robinson Crusoe*?**

ANSWER: *Robinson Crusoe*'s Preface was doubtless written last, when Defoe could survey the book's course. It stresses the story's religious meaning, and the evidence suggests that Defoe wished his hero to undergo moral as well as physical trials. Crusoe, as a full human being, must evolve spiritually, as well as survive physically, and it is this aspect which Defoe recommended to his readers equally with the variety of Crusoe's adventures.

Defoe called the book 'allegorical', probably because, within the adventures, it carries a moral version of life (whether his own life, or life generally). Though many readers take it merely as colourful romance, Crusoe from the start suggests some strange inner meaning, concerning his 'sin' of disobedience. But is this 'sin' more than natural youthful independence? Crusoe thinks that it is, because he owes his father the veneration God means children to feel for parents, and the 'middle state' which his father praises carries God's approval. Crusoe therefore thinks himself not healthily self-reliant but blamably self-willed, and deserving of punishment. The sea-captain takes the storm for 'a plain and visible token' of God's anger.

Years of 'wickedness' are supposed to follow. Of these there is no sign, but the redeemed Crusoe thinks that to have ignored religion and lived a self-directed life is wickedness enough. He has willingly cut himself off from God: he is unwillingly cast away to bring him back to obedience.

He is brought back, uncertainly at first but increasingly, by severe experiences and by reflecting on mercies. He feels God dealing personally with him: the storm is a 'plain token', and on the island he thinks that God's 'distinguishing goodness' has 'singled [him] out', though why he alone survives is something explainable only by God's mysterious plan.

Suffering from ague, he repents the 'uncommon wickedness' which 'provoked the justice of God'. Later, seeing the footprint, he thinks that his landing on the island's safer side means some special providence saving him for a divine purpose. Bible texts help him, though at first he lacks conviction—'the word had no sound'. Grateful 'transports' alternate with neglect: the sprouting barley first seems miraculous, then merely natural. But the barley, earthquake, hurricane, and dream move him toward conversion. In great distress he prays fervently for the first time, asks himself about God's power, and decides that 'deliverance from sin' far outweighs 'deliverance from affliction'.

At last, believing 'everything ordered for the best', he trusts in God, though for a while the footprint frightens him into uncertainty. With assurance renewed, he converts Friday, and 'a secret joy' floods his soul.

Not every reader finds this impressive. Yet several passages ring with emotion. Crusoe's religious terror after his sickness and dream, and his sense of God's power, are earnest and intense; the Bible's messages strike him personally; his sense of God's presence after his loneliness, and his religious happiness after his fear, are exultant; and both the quiet consolations and the passionate raptures of faith are deeply felt, as in his joy over Friday's salvation, or his thankful tears on sailing for home. He has come to recognise 'the secret hand of Providence'. Writing as powerful as this should prove that the moral and religious content is not superficial. However intent Defoe was on imagining the island adventures, he was moved also by the theme of a soul finding its spiritual allegiance.

NOTES: The essay plan is:

(*i*) to find a starting-point in Defoe's intentions;
(*ii*) to admit that not everyone sees a moral or religious aim;
(*iii*) to survey the evidence for religious development;
(*iv*) to move towards a climax;
(*v*) to point throughout to details in the book, and support the discussion with brief, apt quotations;
(*vi*) to end with a brief, firm statement of the conclusion.

QUESTION: Is Defoe in *Robinson Crusoe* 'simply a narrator of plain facts'?

ANSWER: *Robinson Crusoe's* preface asserts that it is 'a just history of fact', with no 'appearance of fiction'. Certainly the appeal of its facts is powerful. It takes us through adventures the very nature of which is not to be mysterious, or veiled in romantic suggestion, but to be hard-headed dealings with a world of real things. The quotation in the question suggests two or three assumptions: first, that plain facts are the book's substance; second, that they are all it contains; and third, that they are offered without any colouring. The answer must discuss these three assumptions.

That plain facts abound is clear. The first sentence—'I was born in the year 1632 in the city of York' and so on—could not be more plainly factual: the last paragraph, summarising what happened later on the island, is less definite but still points clearly to supposed actual events, not romantically glamourised, and spiced only by hints of 'surprising incidents'. Between beginning and end we advance through a firmly factual world—storms and calms at sea, realistic dangers and struggles, and variations of fortune (often defined by reckonings of money, goods, and projects; Defoe delights in specifying cargoes, balance-sheets, debts, and settlements). Such facts might occur in any trading ledger. What have appealed more are the facts of Crusoe's island life, so convincing by their directness and simplicity—his making and furnishing his 'castle', his efforts in tending his goats, his craft in fashioning tools and pots, baking bread, and shaping canoes, his records of island features and ocean currents. Many of the most striking episodes are those best documented with facts, as when Crusoe is salvaging goods from the wreck. We follow, fascinated, every detail of his finds and his measures for securing them.

But the book offers much more than the plain narration of facts. Crusoe's character itself, though as firmly given as the material elements of his existence, is too strongly dramatised not to be more than 'plain fact'. He is resolute and resourceful but also sensitive and thoughtful. From his early rebellious impulses through all the excitements of adventure, from the mysterious urges which drive him to risk everything, when patient persistence would serve better, through the self-examination these urges prompt in him, leading to remorse for 'sin' and to faith in God, he shows himself not a mere practical man but a many-sided (and often very individual) human being.

Nor is his story one merely of 'plain' item-by-item record. He reacts to experience with a striking range of feeling. The early sessions with his father sound a grave and moving note. His rebellion is performed in a spirit of jaunty recklessness. In the first sea-storm he feels the depths of alarm; later, struggling ashore on the island, he exerts a desperate vigour rewarded by an overpowering sense of relief. His varying despairs and hopes on the island form dramas of strong feeling, on one hand 'the melancholy relation of a scene of silent life', on the other the 'great pleasure to see all my goods in such order'. He suffers from ague, is terrified by storms, the earthquake, and the footprint in the sand, and when aided by the company of Friday and other allies shows himself capable of warm feeling. He also gets on goodhearted terms with friends and business associates, and generally he figures as a considerate, likeable man.

Clearly, then, it is not only through plain facts that *Robinson Crusoe* has so widely appealed. They are a basic constituent, which can seize even the youngest or least experienced reader. But Defoe has enriched them with a character study so remarkable that his hero has virtually become a figure of legend, and with a wealth of feeling which causes warm human blood to run in the factual veins.

NOTES: The essay plan is:
   (*i*) to make clear just what the question is asserting;
   (*ii*) to examine the evidence for the assertion;
   (*iii*) to suggest two main amendments to the assertion;
   (*iv*) to arrange the argument with increasing force;
   (*v*) to keep close to the book's contents throughout;
   (*vi*) to sum up, crisply stating the conclusion reached.

QUESTION: **Why has *Robinson Crusoe* appealed so widely?**

ANSWER: Since its publication *Robinson Crusoe* has captured readers' imaginations not only throughout England but widely overseas too. It has kept its popularity even in the different conditions of the twentieth century and in lands Defoe never knew. Crusoe has become almost a mythical character, who sums up qualities and experiences widely felt to represent mankind at large. The book appeals not by offering a world of fantasy, like, say, *The Arabian Nights' Entertainments*, but by presenting a normal man in situations which, though not themselves normal, are thoroughly credible and interesting.

This wide appeal is due to two main qualities. First, there is the humanity of Crusoe himself. Second, his adventures have a double appeal; firstly, they satisfy the widespread yearning for escape from humdrum existence and for the testing of one's courage amid dangers, and secondly they satisfy these desires for novelty and challenge by taking us not into a never-never world but into realistic difficulties and hazards to be tackled by resourceful, practical means. There are no dragons to be faced, no magic wands to be waved. Instead, a shelter must be built, food found, basic tools made, sanity preserved, cannibals and mutineers confronted. Thrown destitute and sea-soaked onto an unknown shore, where perils may lurk behind every bush, and where escape, unlikely at best, depends on courage and enterprise, what will the castaway do? Obviously he survives, otherwise he would not be telling his story. But how?

Defoe might treat all this in a bare, prosaic way. In a sense, much of *Robinson Crusoe* is bare, prosaic fact. We learn of the stores he stows on the Turkish launch when escaping from Sallee, of the goods and money he receives from the Portuguese captain (including the sale price of Xury), his transactions with merchants and planters, the goods and tools salvaged from the wreck, the planks, pots, tools, and clothes he makes, and the profits his Brazilian estate brings. Yet the account is seldom bare and prosaic, for it is always related with a vivid sense of how much it means to Crusoe, and what efforts and emotions it has called for. Hardly has the story begun with the bare facts of his birth and family than it offers the moving drama of his disagreement with his father, a situation readers can readily share in imagination. The excitements of his sea-voyages follow, culminating in his island life. The keynote to the story is adventure, not merely the facts of seafaring and island life, interesting though these are. Whatever the details, they are warmed by the stimulus of danger and enterprise. The making of fences, utensils, clothes and the rest not merely records things done, it is charged with the challenge of tackling new tasks, gaining experience, hoping and fearing for success. How can a man live merely by his own efforts?

Island life might become a monotonous routine. Defoe varies it with dramatic episodes—illness, storm, earthquake; these are not oversensationalised but remain likely and natural occurrences. The drama reaches its climax in the sight of the footprint, and the following dangers of cannibals and mutineers. Through all this Crusoe not only acts but reflects, showing himself an enquiring and humane man. He explores religious problems, broods on differing customs and morals, and shows a shrewd, sound nature to his fellow creatures. These are thoughts and actions we vividly share.

So the book's appeal owes something to our longing for new experience, something to adventures so lifelike that we share them as if they were our own, and something to our fellow feelings for so thoroughly human a character as Crusoe who carries us with him, convinced, in all he feels, thinks, and does.

NOTES: The essay plan is:

(*i*) to define the question's bearing (since its topic is not contentious);
(*ii*) to settle two main areas for demonstration and proof;
(*iii*) to present various elements of appeal;
(*iv*) to suggest how the appeal strengthens as the story proceeds;
(*v*) to refer frequently to actual occurrences;
(*vi*) to sum up with a reminder of what has been shown.

QUESTION: **Which two or three episodes would you recommend as favourable samples of** *Robinson Crusoe*, **and why?**

ANSWER: *Robinson Crusoe* offers many gripping episodes. Though certain general themes bind it together, such as Crusoe's developing experience and his serious reflections, gripping episodes make up its very nature. Defoe engrosses us by the conviction with which he creates strong scenes.

Three which reflect the book's range are those covering the salvage from the wreck, Crusoe's 'terrible dream' while ill, and the rescue of the Spanish captain and Friday's father. These three display respectively the zest of initiative, the force of emotion, and the daring of action.

The first starts with Crusoe finding that the night storm has driven the ship within reach. He weeps to think how near to safety were his fellow sailors, but his grief does not prevent him from planning to profit by his chances. There is a brisk sense of discovery about all this. For instance, only on his second swim round the wreck does he see the rope which lets him climb aboard. He companionably invites us to explore the ship with him—'You may be sure my first work was to search'—and we see him gathering timbers and making his raft. He sets to work, meeting each difficulty, and telling us what commodities he chose for loading (even to the detail of three Dutch cheeses and five pieces of goat's flesh), and how he stows them. Disappointments await him as well as satisfactions; the rats have eaten the barley. The flowing tide takes him by surprise and floats his clothes away, but he finds others, together with arms and ammunition. These he carefully records, together with the numbers of saws of other tools.

Will he get them ashore? Things at first go well, but the raft grounds and nearly spills its cargo: the strain of saving it is vividly conveyed, with the very feel of muscular struggle. All this is told in direct, practical fashion. The businesslike search and the tense effort come through uncoloured, but clearly and strongly.

The terrifying dream works differently. It too is vivid, with its apparition descending in flame from a black cloud, to a Crusoe ill and still alarmed by the earthquake and hurricane. But it is vivid less in a factual way than in a poetically imaginative one. Much is done by power of impression; the earth seems to tremble; the vision is 'inexpressibly dreadful' and speaks with a terrible voice. 'The horrors of my soul', Crusoe says, are impossible to describe, yet we sense them and realise how they stir him to examine his conscience and conduct. The excitements of salvage were physically stirring; the disturbances the vision causes are psychological and disclose depths in Crusoe which neither he nor we had expected.

The rescue of the Spanish captain and Friday's father returns us to adventure excitement but heightens the practical ardour of the salvage by a keen sense of strategy, and a dramatic edginess of timing. Phrases like 'I had now not a moment to lose' keep us on the alert. The episode starts with the stealthy prowl through the woods; we react to each moment of reconnaissance just as Crusoe and Friday do. The scene is closely described—the viewpoints and distances, the critical emergency since the 'poor Christian' is about to be killed, the instructions to Friday, the shooting, and the alarm of the cannibals. Things happen fast, throughout a turbulent scene which yet remains clear and vivid. Crusoe sometimes uses the present tense for immediate effect—'he sees me cock and present', and 'I see them all fall of a heap'.

The Spaniard is saved; a moment of deep relief occurs before the vigorous action is resumed; then the cannibals are routed and the final surprise sprung. Friday's father is discovered, and this leads to a touchingly passionate reunion. So the scene combines physical daring, exciting strategies and surprises, deep feelings, and dramatic moment-by-moment timing, in a fine total effect.

It is clear, then, that Defoe is not a writer with one method of narration only. Other scenes would reveal still further abilities;. but these three may serve to show something of his range, which is a source of vigorous and varying interest in his story.

NOTES: The essay plan is:

(*i*) to explain how episodes are of special value in Defoe's work;
(*ii*) to select examples not only for their own qualities but to illustrate Defoe's range;
(*iii*) to examine each methodically to bring out its nature;
(*iv*) to arrange the three from the simplest to the most complex, for a sense of climax;
(*v*) to keep closely to the text;
(*vi*) to relate the demonstration to Defoe's capacities.

Part 5

Suggestions for further reading

Texts

Many editions in many languages have followed upon the first printing in 1719. The handiest for general modern use is that used for this study, edited by Angus Ross for the Penguin English Library, published (1965) by Penguin Books, Harmondsworth, Middlesex, England, Penguin Books Inc., 3300 Clipper Hill Road, Baltimore 11, Maryland, USA, and Penguin Books Ltd, Ringwood, Victoria, Australia.

Scholarly editions with introductions and good annotations are those edited by J. Donald Crowley in the Oxford English Novels series, Oxford University Press, London, 1972, and Michael Shinagel for the Norton Critical Editions series, W.W. Norton, New York, 1975. Useful inexpensive editions are those in the Everyman's Library, Dent and Dutton, London and New York, 1906 and later—this contains the *Farther Adventures* too—and the Signet Classics, New American Library, New York, 1960. The *Serious Reflections* (along with the *Vision of the Angelick World*) is seldom reprinted but exists in a reprint by Constable, London, 1925.

Other works by Defoe

Letters, edited by G.H. Healey, Clarendon Press, Oxford, 1951
Moll Flanders, Everyman's Library, Dent and Dutton, London and New York, 1930 (and later); edited by Juliet Mitchell, Penguin English Library, Harmondsworth, Middlesex, England, 1978
Roxana, the Fortunate Mistress, edited by Jane Jack, Oxford English Novels series, Oxford University Press, London, 1964
Daniel Defoe: Selected Writings, edited by J.T. Boulton, Batsford, London, 1965, and Cambridge University Press, London, 1975
The Best of Defoe's 'Review', edited by W.L. Payne, Columbia University Press, New York, 1951
Tour Through the Whole Island of Great Britain, edited by G.D.H. Cole and D.C. Browning, Everyman's Library, Dent and Dutton, London and New York, 1962

General reading

BYRD, MAX (ED.): *Twentieth-Century Views: Daniel Defoe*, Prentice-Hall, Englewood Cliffs, New Jersey, USA, 1976. A good collection of critical essays.

CLIFFORD, J.L. (ED.): *Pope and His Contemporaries*, Clarendon Press, Oxford, 1949. Contains a discussion of Defoe's style by Bonamy Dobree, 'Aspects of Defoe's Prose'

DOTTIN, PAUL: *The Life and Strange and Surprising Adventures of Daniel Defoe*, Stanley Paul, London, 1928. Somewhat outmoded, but useful for its wide survey of the time.

EARLE, PETER: *The World of Defoe*, Weidenfeld and Nicolson, London, 1976. Interesting social history, with chapters on 'The Inner World' and 'The Wider World' giving good background to the novels.

ELLIS, FRANK H. (ED.): *Twentieth-Century Interpretations of 'Robinson Crusoe'*, Prentice-Hall, Englewood Cliffs, New Jersey, USA, 1969. A good collection of modern critical essays.

LINNERT, GUSTAV L.: *An Investigation into the Language of 'Robinson Crusoe'*, Almqvist and Wiksell, Uppsala, 1910. A thorough linguistic study.

MOORE, J.R.: *Daniel Defoe: Citizen of the Modern World*, University of Chicago Press, 1958. A full biography, with a *Robinson Crusoe* chapter relating the novel well to Defoe's interests.

ROGERS, PAT (ED.): *Defoe: the Critical Heritage*, Routledge and Kegan Paul, London, 1972. An excellent introduction to and anthology of Defoe criticism.

SECORD, A.W.: *Studies in the Narrative Method of Defoe*, University of Illinois Press, 1924. Good on the book's relationship to travel narratives.

STARR, G.A.: *Defoe and Spiritual Autobiography*, Princeton University Press, 1965. This deals well with Defoe's spiritual precursors.

SUTHERLAND, JAMES R.: *Daniel Defoe: a Critical Study*, Houghton, Mifflin, Inc, Boston, Mass, 1971. The best biographical and critical study.

Defoe, Methuen, London, 1937. An earlier but still useful biography.

Defoe, British Council and Longman Group, London, 1970. A good pamphlet-length introduction.

TILLYARD, E.M.W.: *The Epic Strain in the English Novel*, Chatto and Windus, London, 1958. Sensitively analyses Defoe's communicative vitality.

WATT, IAN: *The Rise of the Novel*, Chatto and Windus, London, 1957. An excellent discussion of Defoe's significance.

The author of these notes

PROFESSOR ARTHUR HUMPHREYS was educated at St Catharine's College, Cambridge, and Harvard University. He was a Supervisor in English at the University of Cambridge; Lecturer in English, University of Liverpool; and British Council Lecturer in English, University of Istanbul before becoming Professor of English at the University of Leicester in 1947. He has been a Fellow of the Folger Library, Washington, on three occasions. His publications include: *William Shenstone* (1937); The *Augustan World* (1954); *Steele, Addison and their periodical essays* (1959); and *Melville* (1962). He has edited Shakespeare's *Henry IV* parts 1 & 2 (1960; 1966); *Joseph Andrews* (1962); *Tom Jones* (1962); *Amelia* (1963); *Jonathan Wild* (1964); *Whitejacket* (1966); Shakespeare's *Richard the Second* (1967), *Henry V* (1968) and *Henry VIII* (1971). He has also contributed to various learned journals and is at present a guest Professor in Turkey.

Escaping Bohemia

Sophia Moseley

Copyright © 2020 Sophia Moseley

All rights reserved, including the right to reproduce this book, or portions thereof in any form. No part of this text may be reproduced, transmitted, downloaded, decompiled, reverse engineered, or stored, in any form or introduced into any information storage and retrieval system, in any form or by any means, whether electronic or mechanical without the express written permission of the author.

The views expressed in this work are solely those of the author and do not necessarily reflect the views of the publisher, and the publisher hereby disclaims any responsibility for them.

ISBN: 9798678661487

Introduction

I became bored of using my excuses! So I decided to exorcise them with the power of the pen; well, iPad actually!

Ah! The delightful memories of childhood fill our hearts and minds with love and joy, as a kind knowing smile glides across our lips, surrounding our whole body with a protective aura, that is invisible to the human eye.

These wonderful memories of our childhood and the fulfilling experiences that we encountered make us into well-rounded, capable adults that can give greatness back to society and anything less than a fabulous start in life makes us less of a being. A being that should just hide in the shadows, rolling along with whatever life and other people decide to throw our way.

Well, this is what society had led me to believe, *or did I* just allow myself to believe that and then hide behind that untruth? I really don't know but what I do know is that I wasted a lot of my life and my magic, my potential, believing that I was less, less than I should be, less than I could be, less than *you* and every other human.

I hid from my childhood, as if I were a child hiding from a monster under the bed. I stayed tight under my duvet afraid to take a peek at the dark monstrous mess that lurked underneath me but at the same time surrounded me. I thought that if I let this beast out of its hiding place, society wouldn't allow me to be well-rounded, capable or a valued woman able to be a good mother or contribute to a world of perfection. I believed that I would be judged harshly, that I would be unlikeable and certainly unlovable, if my dirty childhood secrets came to light.

So instead of confronting the monster that had blighted my childhood, tearing it to shreds, putting it in the furnace and watching it disappear from my present and my future, I decided to stuff it into a bag and carry it around with me, for a long, long time. It may have been invisible but it was there, heavy on my back and in my heart, reminding me who I was, what I could achieve, or more accurately not achieve, even dream of achieving and what I should accept from life and those that I encountered.

Whenever the conversation arose about childhood, parents and the good old days, I would mostly try not to delve into the past, particularly with anyone who didn't know me as a child. And even those that knew me well, I chose not to share any of those secrets that made me feel like I didn't deserve to be.

"My childhood was a little bohemian," I would offer; this wasn't a lie, as such. It was embellished, though; in fact it was me shaking a whole lot of glitter over a turd!

I would then endeavour to direct the conversation in a different direction or wholeheartedly listen to others' beautiful tales of perfect parents and summer holidays filled with childlike mischief, which, of course, always made me feel intense jealousy.

A series of events and encounters led me to the point of admitting to myself that my childhood was not only bohemian, it was a lot more than that and less than a childhood. It was a whole different world away from my life now and the life that I try to give my own precious daughters. These encounters slowly, gently and kindly persuaded me that I should release the monster from the bag, that by doing so it would no longer hold any power on or over me. I would no longer be consumed by the shame and guilt that were like my imaginary friends, and kept me in check all these years, making sure that I didn't make silly mistakes by thinking that I could do anything too extraordinary or wonderful.

So here, in this safe place, I gently ease open the bag and allow the monster to escape from its long slumber, one memory at a time, until its once resting place is free from its weight and I'm free from its grasp!

Are you coming with me on this bumpy, dark ride? *I may need a friend.*

The Beast Ejects the Baby

I hear crying and screaming, then banging and shouting. There's a whirl of emotions that are uncomfortably palatable. I know what's happened straight away. He's chucked the little baby and cot in the hall once again. Her little pleading wails pierce my young heart but for the moment there is nothing that I can do, I must wait silently and patiently, even though hearing this unfold is making me want to vomit.

"Will this cruel madness ever end?" I whisper.

I've always understood that babies cry; they have needs and to communicate their needs they cry. Even as a child, I knew this to be a fact because I cried, even as a teen. However, I cried and no one met my needs and it seemed that the same was happening to the baby. She was so small, still in a cot, still vulnerable and in need of so much more from these adults; she wasn't yet as resilient as me, but she would be, she would have to be.

"Why the fuck won't she shut up? All night she just whines… Shut the fuck up, brat!" the big brute yelled as he towered over the cot now residing in the hallway. He stood there just in his boxer shorts, large gut hanging over them with his hands gripping the cot still. The sweet baby inside going pink in the face and flailing her tiny arms around as she screamed, pleading to be picked up. How could an adult not feel empathy for this little being, who just wanted to be held?

He might as well have been banging his chest because he was certainly acting like a wild beast. I witnessed all of this as I peered through the crack in my bedroom door. I would have to wait until he stopped having his little boy tantrum to go and collect her. This is where sleeping together began, me protecting her from the noise of this flat and showing her the love that a human being needs and should give.

I do not know what crime she had committed that night, hungry, toothache, ill, but whatever it was 'the parents' weren't in the mood to deal with it. Obviously, being selfish drunks and having children doesn't go hand in hand.

My mother didn't make any attempt to leave the bedroom to protect her daughter. Either she was so drunk that she didn't realise what was happening or she thought it was best not to get involved, so the evening didn't progress into violence. Whatever the reason, I was beginning to hate her more each day for not being a mother and protecting her children.

At this point, Jemma was crying more forcefully, waving her arms around desperately in need of comfort. She didn't know what was going on, she just wanted love, she wanted to be held.

"Oh God, I'm going to lose my temper soon!" he barked.

I could have laughed at this if it wasn't such a crap situation. He probably thought he was as cool as a cucumber and that this was parenting at its finest. I didn't laugh, though, or make any noise. I just waited and waited, for what seemed like an eternity. I got used to waiting as I grew up, I was always waiting for something.

Still there was silence from the bedroom, no movement, nothing. Maybe she was dead! *Come on, anything's a possibility, here*, I thought. Though I was not worried for her.

He shoved the huge cot a little further down the hall, away from their room. He snarled at the baby and turned back towards their bedroom and he slammed the door so hard a picture fell off the wall, which shook my baby sister into silence, her little face in an expression of pure terror; she looked ready to burst into an ear-shattering scream at any minute.

It was at this point I stuck my head around my door and just motioned for her to remain hushed. I must wait just a few moments so he doesn't reappear, else I would just get punished as well and that would serve no one.

Her delightful little face lights up when she sees me, she knows she will receive some tenderness now, whatever the original problem was, it doesn't matter now because we have each other.

After waiting for a few tense minutes, I walked into the hall and scooped her up. I loved cuddling her. Since she was born, I hadn't felt so alone or sad. Now I must be mature and make sure she is okay.

I took this little wonder to the kitchen, as she clung tightly to my nightie and gazed at me with love. I put a little milk in a bottle for her, it would fill her tummy, which was no doubt empty and the cause of her pleading; to me it seemed so simple. She also had a soaking nappy that was bulging through her baby-grow, any idiot could see that, I thought, with anger in my heart for that cruel bastard that happened to be her father, in name if not in actions.

After carrying her to my room, grabbing a nappy on the way, I cleaned her up, as best I could, and put on a fresh nappy – nappies really weren't my top skill! I then snuggled her in bed with her bottle. I held her close all night and she made contented sounds, like the cat that got the cream. Actually, I felt like the lucky one, at last I have a friend amongst all this madness.

It wasn't long after this that she was moved to my room, which made it a lot easier for me to care for her and, of course, made me feel less lonely, in a home that always seemed filled with so much loneliness, even when there were always people around.

Looking back on this event, I know that it cemented my love and empathy for others within my life. It made me realise that there would be times when I would need to be strong for the sake of those around me. I'm thankful that my small baby sister taught me how to love and give unselfishly, how to love without expecting anything in return.

I Was Never Invited to the Party

The darkness of the sky matched the darkness I felt in my heart. Cold, dark pain that was closing in on me. It felt like I would never escape the darkness, it had a strong grip on my young body and mind. However, I always felt an expanse of possibilities as I gazed at the stars above me, always sleeping with the curtains open. I lay there staring up, out into the world, knowing there was something better than this. The little twinkling stars gave me hope; I smiled as I drifted off to that place.

It seemed like only seconds had passed and the front door flew open, crashing against the wall. The draft caused my bedroom door to drift open and then the noise began. I knew I had little hope for sleep now. There would be an all-night party that children were certainly not invited to, though we would be subjected to it.

"We need some music!" a familiar voice shouted.

"You know where the radio is, it's not moved, you lazy shit!" my mother retorted.

In the lower bunk, my baby sister stirred. I slowly and very quietly slipped out of the top bunk and snuggled in with her; heaven forbid anyone heard me and realised that we were awake and came in our room. She was so sweet and I held her in my arms, hoping I could protect her from the onslaught of music, shouting and laughing that no doubt would go on for hours.

"Let's get this fucking party started, where's the drink?" came the man's voice. "You want some of this? It's good stuff, keep you going for days!"

There was a scream of laughter. Sounded like a houseful tonight. I guessed I wouldn't make school again tomorrow. I would be too tired again after listening to this insane noise all night. At least I could keep this little angel asleep.

Nights like this were commonplace and it seemed that no one had any concern about children that needed to go to school the next day. My mother would always have the radio playing, twenty-four hours a day. She didn't like to be on her own and silence was too loud for her, so the radio was her company when her cronies weren't around. The muffled sounds from the kitchen kept me awake until she fell asleep and I could turn it down or off. When she had people round, they ramped up the volume so they could hear it in the living room, while they steadily got more and more hammered. I would hide my head under my pillow, waiting for them to leave. I hated noise, peace was all that I yearned for and now I'm still a terribly light sleeper, I hardly ever have a full night's sleep.

This particular party went on and on, screaming and laughing filled the flat until the birds started singing and the sun made an appearance, which on this occasion was not welcome by me; I wanted and needed sleep. I was a growing teenager with hormones racing round, sleep was much needed.

As light started to stream into the bedroom, a few people left and some started to snore in the living room, which was next to my bedroom. My mother and someone disappeared into her bedroom. I could hear them giggling with excitement. It seemed like she had forgotten that she had children, once again, and that we may need, oh I don't know… to get to school.

It seemed to me as a child that most adults, except a few, were innately selfish and self-absorbed. They came first, at all times, and life was for them, all about having fun, even if that came at a cost. Watching these adults live their addiction-fuelled lives made me make a concerted effort to be mindful of those around me. I tried hard to put others first, to be totally unselfish. This sounds like some saintly quality, however what I've realised as I ponder that once turbulent time, is *yes!* It's wonderful to think of others and not to be consumed by oneself but when it allows others to walk all over you or it is a reason for you not to chase your dreams, then it becomes a hindrance, an excuse, a burden. That benefits no one, not you and certainly not your loved ones.

Now I'm learning to be less selfish-less, not in a way that my mother was, but in a way that my soul dictates and allows me to follow my dreams, and not to be constantly in the service of others. Because it's okay to put myself first sometimes.

The Butcher's Knife

It was gone twelve that night; we had been sleeping peacefully. The flat had been extremely quiet that evening and we had gone to bed with a feeling of calm.

I didn't expect to see my mum until some time the next day; I just had a feeling when she went out that she would be away for a while. It wasn't just a night down the pub or clubbing in town, her and her pals were up to no good. I became very good at reading the signs, in fact reading people.

Our flat was surrounded by old people, poor buggers having us as neighbours. There was never any noise unless we made it. So, when I heard the metal bins in the garden clattering, I knew that it was something to be scared of. There was trouble and it would be directed our way, for sure.

I was already an extremely light sleeper due to my mum's comings and goings. As I left our bedroom to go and investigate, I was shaking, my heart was beating so fast, I thought it would jump out of the nightie I was wearing. A nightie that I had owned for years that read "I am ten" and I most definitely was not ten! I really wasn't a cool teenager!

As I pulled the bedroom door shut and started down the hallway, the front door burst open and in ran three large, dirty yobs. I ran back to our room. The noise had woken my sister and she was now standing by the bunk beds, looking as petrified as I felt, though I tried hard not to show it. Show no fear! Always show no fear! That had already become my mantra, even though at that time I had no idea what a mantra was.

One of the 'men' – and I use that term very loosely – grabbed me and started to pull and push me around. He pushed me to the floor and then dragged me back up, slapped me a few times, all while my terrified little sister stood frozen watching; she didn't move a muscle. Neither of us made a sound, though, no pleading, crying or anything.

I heard the other two in our front room. I guessed that they would be helping themselves to my mum's treasures. All I can remember feeling is pure rage and a strong feeling that I must protect my sister.

"How fucking dare they, who the heck do they think they are?" raced through my head on repeat and I could feel the anger build up inside of me as I got pushed and pulled around. I think the anger pushed out any fear that I may have felt. I wanted to hurt these men, who thought that it was okay to abuse us this way.

By this point, I was seriously starting to tire of this calibre of my mother's associates. I was starting to be filled with a fire that wouldn't be put out for years because of my pure hatred for that way of life and the people who seemed to enjoy it.

I managed to free myself from this delinquent idiot and I took a risk as I fled from the room and rushed to the kitchen. Luckily, he followed me and left my sister alone. My mother had acquired a butcher's meat cleaver that was hanging near the kitchen door, which I grabbed. I rushed towards him, as the other two sauntered out of the front room, holding loot, like a couple of fat pirates without the charm. I was swinging the cleaver and screaming, all seven stone of me.

"Get out, get out, get out!" That's all I could say, no swearing, nothing else. I was so crazy my brain couldn't find any other words. I knew one thing for sure, I would not allow these arseholes any more fun and games.

I must have looked a sight. This small teenage girl in a nightie, swinging a knife, screaming. So, they were either scared I was going to use it as I nearly did get them a few times, or they had what they had come for, because they hastily left.

The latch on the door had broken off but luckily there was a bolt at the top of the door, which I pulled across swiftly. I also managed to push a chair up against the door, but the truth be told, this would have served no purpose. I then proceeded to make sure the back door was locked and all the windows were shut. There were no locks on those, though. It made me feel better, even just a little, by taking back some kind of control of our home.

Then after placing the cleaver under the pillow, we climbed into bed and tried to sleep as we held each other. In truth, I spent the night replaying the scene over and over in my mind, trying to not imagine what else could have happened. I suspect my little sister had the episode visit her several times in her sleep over the years, trying to make sense of it.

This is when sleeping with a knife under my pillow and a baseball bat by the door began. I did this every time I lived on my own, until I was about thirty-five. I know, totally crazy. I can just see raised eyebrows! My husband was slightly scared when he first met me. I have to admit that it is a pretty frightening scene for a new romantic interest: a baseball bat by the door and a knife under the pillow. I'm just imagining the horrifying scene now. Other than that, I must have seemed quite normal because he didn't seem that bothered by my weapons of war.

That fateful night no neighbours came to see what all the noise was about, no one felt the need to check that two children were safe. I didn't even consider reporting it to the police, as they only ever visited our flat to arrest my mum or look for someone and, dare I say it, to find out any information that they may need.

When my mum returned the next day, she didn't even bat an eyelid at what had happened; just one of those things. These kind of things happened all the time, you don't report it, you get your own back at a later date, if you can.

She was mighty upset about the fact that one of the items that had been taken was an antique knife. It was the kind of curved knife that Nepalese Gurkhas used in combat, a Khufu Rui, I believe. My mum had owned it for as long as I could remember. I believe it was a gift, maybe from before I was born.

That was probably the only item stolen that night that wasn't stolen on a previous occasion; it sounds weird even saying it. My mum was deeply upset by its loss and I never found out why it meant so much to her.

I don't know if my mum ever got her revenge on those thugs, either. I would say she did even if it was years later. I often think of my mother's treasure and where it ended up. I found it quite sad that it was taken as I remember playing with it as a youngster and how fond she was of it. I hope that someone eventually owned it that appreciated its value and beauty.

That evening is still very real in my mind; the feelings of fear and anger all swirling round in my body and the intense feeling that I must protect even though it was over thirty years ago. I'm so thankful that the event didn't evolve into even more violence and that our pain wasn't greater. I know that we were blessed that they left our home when they did.

I learnt that evening that I had an inner strength that I could call on in times of trouble. Throughout my life, I've sometimes forgotten how strong and powerful I had been on that evening and I have allowed people to walk all over me since. I'm extremely thankful for the memory of that girl and the strength she showed that evening, and I intend to honour her by always remembering to be strong in situations that may make my knees quake.

Fagin Taught Me Well

I sat in the hallway, crouched on the floor leaning back on the wall. I dozed in and out of the sleep that I desperately yearned for but I must listen for the sounds of sleep coming from the other room.

At that moment it was other sounds that came from my mum's room, sounds of animalistic pleasure. It made me cringe and I felt quite nauseated, a child listening to her mum have sex, not an activity I would have chosen, for sure.

The flat was always full of some kind of noise; people, music, shouting, laughter. It wasn't often noise coming from us kids, though. This is probably one of the reasons that I like quiet now or the sounds of nature. Background noises just drive me crazy.

Eventually the sound of snoring started to drift from the bedroom. It began as a low rumble drifting slowly through the air but rapidly it changed into a pig-like roar of some crazed hog.

I started to edge towards the bedroom, still low to the ground on all fours like a dog. Actually, I felt lower than a dog, not that I thought dogs were particularly low on the scale of lowness. In my mind, I had met many humans that could take the title of lowest being on the planet.

As I approached the door, which was open just a crack, my heart started to beat super fast, my hands were clammy and I remembered how much I hated doing this. I cautiously eased the door open further and peered around the door. I had become an expert in making no noise. I knew all the creaks in the flat and I could control my breathing and keep it extremely light.

As always, they were both sound asleep. I stared at them for a while, entwined, disgusting bodies and faces that were puffed with years of abuse. My mum was closest to the door, with her lover next to the wall but still facing me. The whole scene repulsed me... they repulsed me... *she really repulsed me!*

I stayed low to the floor, practically on my belly, sliding like a snake. I felt my whole body shaking as I tried to get this task over as soon as possible. My nerves were totally shredded; this was too much stress.

I reached the pile of clothes in the corner of the room. It didn't take long to find his large trousers in the pile. There was a little clattering as I removed them from the other garments; it was the change in his pocket, about to give me away. I turned and checked that they were still fast asleep. Yep, thank God. My heart and my breathing were getting faster and faster. I started to sweat as I turned back to the pile of clothes and the task in hand. I don't think an atomic bomb would have woken their drunk arses up anyway, but that didn't do anything to help the fear subside at the time.

I slipped my hand into the back pocket and pulled out a large brown leather wallet. It felt really heavy. As I opened it, I felt a little jump for joy. It certainly was brimming with notes, lots of notes. I had always been instructed not to take too much but enough to make it worth it, getting caught that is!

"Make it count!" I could hear her voice in my head.

I eased out about a third of the notes that were in there and rolled them into a neat roll and started to make my escape. My excitement started to grow, my job was nearly completed and there was something to show for it.

Will she be pleased with me? I thought. I really hoped that she would. I always wanted her to be pleased with me.

I backed out of the room the way that I came in, on my belly. As I reached the door, I gently pulled it shut as I eased myself out of the room. I slipped into the kitchen and put all of the money except ten pounds into a great big ancient pot on the top shelf. I don't know how much there was, there was a lot for sure, but the ten pounds was a lot to me, and it was my self-payment.

I didn't really know who her friend was or what he did, even though I had met him several times. But, of course, as a child, I didn't need to know anything. I just knew he did have strong feelings for my mother. He would come visiting often. He would pull up in his mauve Jag, take her out, they would get drunk and come back and pass out.

She hadn't always wanted me to fleece him but, of late, this was a new trick she had persuaded me to do. I think at one point she had hoped to have a real relationship with him, but he wouldn't leave his family and she became a little bitter. Or it was just a necessity that we had to undertake. I think on reflection that it was a combination of the two. She had once again hoped for more from the man that she had given her heart to and, as before, so many times, she had been let down.

I'm not sure if her lover ever cottoned on to the missing money. Did he even notice it had gone? Where it had gone? Or did he just believe that he had spent or lost it on their drink-infused date?

My mum always said, "He will never know, he's so pissed, the silly fart."

I just did what I was told at that point. I knew more money meant more food, as well as my mother being happier because she could fuel her alcoholic need.

He was not the only one that got this treatment, but he's the one that I remember most because I actually liked him.

He seemed a decent sort of fella, really, if you overlook him cheating on his wife. He was always kind to me and my sister, he would bring us small gifts and speak kindly to us and my mum. He was a gentle man who didn't cause us any harm, and there is a lot to be said for that... good old-fashioned kindness.

If you can be anything... Be Kind!

Asleep Or... Dead

As I looked into the front room window, she lay as still as a corpse. Was she? Had it actually happened this time?

"Shit," I mumbled out loud, "I can't believe this, Mum. Oh, bloody great, it gets better, another new dickhead to deal with too."

I let this new wave of disappointment wash over me as I took in the facts of this new disaster scene: my mum pissed at 3.30pm on a school day, passed out on the floor with another stranger and I can't get in the house.

The only thing that could make it worse was if they were naked. Thank God they weren't!

"Mum, mum, let me in, mum."

I tap lightly on the window as I try to not draw anyone's attention to the situation. As nosey as the neighbours were, they didn't care and really they just wanted an excuse to get us out.

"Mum!"

The mess of the figure in the room starts to move a little, then more, and as she does, she groans. She struggles to get to her feet as she wobbles several times. The male figure doesn't move a muscle; maybe he is dead. As she eventually stands, she begins to reveal herself as her trousers slowly slip down.

Oh God, my embarrassment is complete.

"I hate you," I silently mumble, mainly to myself.

This 'thing' that I call mother eventually manages to become completely upright and hold onto her trousers as she wobbles towards the door. Still the vile figure upon the floor lays there, lifeless. I hope he's dead, another evil bastard gone, I think!

After what seems like an eternity, as I wait at the front door in the December freeze, in a barely-there coat, she emerges as she creaks the door open.

"For heaven's sake, you're a mess AGAIN, selfish cow!" I blurt out as I try not to smell the stench of urine mixed with that familiar smell of alcohol.

For once it would be nice to come home from school to a cooked meal, a loving mum, no strangers and the pretty lights that I see on in other people's homes as I walk home in the freezing winter rain.

"Oh, someone had a fucking fabulous day at school then!" She cackles at me like one of Macbeth's hags.

I push by her, trying not to cry or be sick at the same time. My heart is broken once again, and I can't hold back the single salty tear that trickles down my cheek. All I want is normality and pure love. I decide that the best course of action is to head towards my bedroom and stay there until it's safe to come out.

As I enter my sanctuary, there's my little sister, sitting on the bed playing with her favourite teddy, my Paddington. The same Paddington Bear whose wellingtons she wears. My pure sweet sister who gives me all the unconditional love that my selfish mother doesn't. My heart breaks for her, as she has to be around this more than I do. At least I get to escape to school.

"Big sis," she screams as she jumps off the bed and stretches up her arms to me.

We embrace and we both know that we will be safe now we are together.

"Hi, lovely. What have you been up to today?" I ask as I hold her close, just as I did when she was a tiny baby.

"I've been to school and then after mummy got me, she said I had to stay in here, so I've been cuddling teddy," she whispers. "There's been lots of noise and I don't like it."

"Don't worry, I'm here now and we can play. We will eat later on, honey, but what shall we play now?"

"Can we play with Grandad's playhouse?" she sweetly asks.

The playhouse was a doll's house that my grandad had made me. It was basic but we thought it was beautiful and we both loved playing with it, even though I was a teenager.

We had allowed the hamster that we briefly owned to live in it. Watching him scamper from room to room until a great big ginger tomcat decided the little critter looked too tasty to resist. There was no chance of saving the poor little beast, even though I did give chase as the cat darted out of the house with his stolen tasty dinner. So, since that sad departure, the house was once again returned to its former glory as a home for our mishmash of dolls.

She loved to play happy families with the little house, with all the tiny furniture that my grandad had lovingly made or my nanny had picked up from the jumble sale. She always played the mother role, who was more often than not cooking something delicious and so super loving to the children dolls. *And in that game were a little girl's hopes and dreams!*

We spent the rest of the afternoon playing and acting out with the dollies, laughing as we made up funny stories and scenarios for our doll actors to act out. It was times like those that kept me sane. Those times helped me block out what was really going on within the walls of our home. Being a normal kid, playing, giggling and having no worries... There's a lot to be said for normality!

We leave our mother to it, whatever *it* is, while we play house with our dolly house and in life, sometimes!

As a teenager, I was always so embarrassed by my mum's behaviour, it cut me to the core. By this point, I really didn't like her, and I couldn't wait to escape. I thought her actions were selfish, calculated and made to hurt me on purpose. With maturity, I can look at this scenario slightly differently: yes she was being selfish but her actions weren't designed to hurt me or drive a wedge between us. She was in pain, a deep pain that was literally eating her from the inside out. No one could help her because she didn't want help, particularly by this stage. She had lost the vision of who she truly was and was rather swiftly becoming who she thought she was. My heart is full of love for her and I wish that someone could have helped her come to terms with the blackness that put her on a course of self-destruction at a very young age.

We should never judge another's life because we don't know the path that they have had to travel. If someone is lacking in strength to make it through a trial, give them some of your strength; they can then choose whether to accept it or not.

Going On Your Holidays, Love?

It was another sunny day. I loved these days, it meant that I could be out of the house away from the madness. I hadn't escaped the madness that day yet, but at least the sky was blue and the sun was already warming the air.

My mother seemed particularly agitated that day. She was pacing the flat, like a caged panther. I could hear her mumbling to herself as she went from room to room, which gave me a stomach-curdling unease; it meant something was coming, that something bad was about to happen. Something was definitely coming and, by the look of her, coming soon straight to our door.

Someone had arrived early at the flat. I had been awoken by a death-awakening bang at the front door, then groans and blasphemous spitting as she opened the door, then about ten minutes of whispering, with the sudden loud "fuck" or "bollocks" thrown in. Yep, something was definitely going on. When things out of the norm started happening around here, there was without a doubt something going to happen, something to be worried about.

"Soph, go get Sadie for me!" she screamed from the kitchen.

I knew better than to argue with my mother when she had morphed into a caged beast; there would be only one outcome and loser in that battle, and it wouldn't be her.

"Tell her that she must come, and *now,* tell her that the shit's going to hit the fan!"

"What if she can't come?" I questioned.

"God, child, make her come, tell her if she wants to avoid trouble to get her fat arse here!" she screamed back at me.

With that, I put on my scruffy white pumps and headed towards the door. My sister was still in her pyjamas snuggled in the chair with a blanket and munching some toast, blissfully unaware that a storm of some sort was heading our way.

I skipped the short distance to Sadie's home and tapped on the door.

"Mum said that she needs you, there's trouble," I sweetly stated.

I left out the swearing and insults, as I thought that they were unnecessary, and I was slightly scared of Sadie and her bullish family. Though they were always nice to us, it was great being friends with a family that no one messes with, a family that always looked out for those that they cared for. It didn't stop me feeling intimidated by them, though.

Her face seemed to go a nice shade of green. As she grabbed a cardigan hanging by the door, she screamed up the stairs, "I'm off up the road, I won't be long. If anyone asks, I'm at the shop!"

There was no answer to her fishwife screams, to which she rolled her eyes and put her hands on her hips as she took a deep breath.

"Hey, did you fucking hear, arsehole?" she now barked.

"Yesss, woman. Shut up!" came the reply down the stairs.

As we enter the flat, the front door is always on the latch, my mother comes rushing out of the front room. Fag in one hand and her little green teacup in the other. She's totally frazzled at this point and swaying a little.

"Do one, piss off!" she glares at me, as I retreat into the front room to be with my sister.

There's lots of whispering, swearing and banging for the next fifteen or so minutes, until suddenly Sadic leaves. As I look out of the window, I watch her slam the gate; she's now carrying a large brown suitcase that looks like it belongs in an Agatha Christie movie. She marches down the road with the full force of a woman on a mission.

Before I even have time to sit back down, there's a commotion outside. As I return my gaze outside, there are police cars swarming down the road and halt outside the flat.

Suddenly it all clicks. "Oh!"

The police officers leap out of the cars, practically jump our fence and bang the door, which of course flies open. I hear it banging against the wall with such a force that I'm sure there will be a huge mark.

"Oh, what's all this, how rude, what's going on? Don't you know I have kids?" I hear my mum's voice, trying to sound surprised.

"Morning, love, we missed you. So, let's have a chat, what have you been up to?" I hear a man's voice reply to my mum.

At this point, a policewoman comes into the front room.

"Right, you two, stay here, don't move an inch," she snarls.

She starts to rummage through the sideboard with no care for any of our special items in there; it's shocking to watch. My darling sister comes and holds me, and we sit and stare in disbelief at what's happening. I hear noises in every room, it must be the other police officers. There's banging, slamming and a lot of loud noises.

After what seems like an age, my mum comes in, kisses us both on the head and walks out of the flat. I watch her go down the path, her hands are handcuffed, and she is being guided by a man in a suit – he looks super important! My stomach does somersaults, and a tear rolls down my face.

With that, Gwen, my mum's good friend, comes in. I like Gwen, she's kind, normal and not an addict or a criminal. She has a husband, two kids and a lovely home on the estate. With her entrance, the last police leave. They seem pleased with their morning's work, with no concern for us children.

"Come on, girls, let's get you to my house."

We collect a few bits, a teddy, cardigans and some clothes to dress my sister in, and leave, locking the door behind us. It's 9.30 in the morning and I am ashamed, angry and shattered.

Years later, I remember my mum and her friend laughing about the day that she took a suitcase from my mum and, when the police stopped her, moments later, their words were, "Going on your holidays, love?"

They laughed and laughed about that. I don't know what happened, but I know that they saw the funny side in getting caught. Now, whenever I'm in the hairdressers and they inevitably say, "Going on your holidays?" I always think about my mum and her friend and the comic value of that scene and many more from that time in my life. Yes, I would have preferred a dad, a mum, one sibling, a Labrador and a Volvo at the time, but I wouldn't have learnt the lessons that I did, grown how I was meant to or had memories like this. Thank you, ladies, for that comic moment on a council estate in England, in the 1980s.

I Watched Him Bleed

I lay in bed listening to the raised voices circling through the rest of the flat. This fight had been going on for at least an hour and it was already 1.30 in the morning. *God how I wish they would give the pub a rest!*

Then on reflection, I guess they would still drink at home, it wouldn't make a blind bit of difference. Though they may fight earlier, which would benefit me and my schooling greatly.

I heard a huge crash as something obviously went flying through the air and landed against a wall. Things seemed to be escalating as there was another crash. This time I heard my mother scream, the banging and crashing continuing around the front room for what seemed like an hour but in reality was only a couple of minutes, then the front room door slammed.

"At least I will be able to sleep now," I whisper to myself, but really my heart was racing and my mind was whizzing around with the scenes that played out in my head to go with the noises I'd just heard.

I then heard a bloodcurdling scream, which in itself wasn't strange, but what was strange and extremely shocking was that it was my stepfather, not my mum.

"What have you done, you bitch?!" he flung at her. "Call an ambulance!"

"Call it your fucking self, arsehole. I'm going to bed!" I heard my mum spit back.

With that, I heard my mum's bedroom door shut and rustling in the kitchen. Then I thought I heard the front door shut, so with that I got up to see what had been going on. However, as I left the safety of my room, I saw my stepfather, that huge beast of a man, standing at the front door with a pair of scissors sticking out of his chest with a dirty tea towel wrapped around them. We stared at each other in complete shock for a brief moment. Him with anger in his eyes, which actually wasn't unusual, and me with panic. I retreated back into my room and swiftly jumped back in bed. What had I just seen? Whatever it was, I knew the best thing to do was to stay where I was and to say nothing at all, to *anyone*.

"I'm going to the phone box to ring the police!" he shouted as he slammed the door.

We had a lovely big red telephone for years; however, it was never connected, just for show. I guess he wished it was connected now, instead of having to walk to the telephone box.

There was no more movement in the flat. I guess my mum had eventually passed out. I stayed awake for what seemed like the remainder of the night, with the image of my stepfather and the scissors sticking out of his large body in my mind.

The next morning, just as I was leaving for school, he returned, patched up. It seemed he had decided not to call the police but instead went to hospital. I presume that some kind of story was fabricated, as she didn't seem to get into any trouble for it, or maybe I missed that. Luckily for them both, it seemed that the scissors had missed anything vital and the fat on his body had protected him somewhat.

It seemed that my mother forgave him for the bruises on her face and the pain in her right arm and he had forgiven her, even though she had plunged scissors into his body. I guess they both realised that they were as guilty as each other. So, for the time being, there was peace and love, that strange kind of love that alcoholics need.

I, on the other hand, decided never to leave my bedroom again if I heard a fuss, fight or any scary noise, as this wasn't the first one of their fights that had escalated. She had already ended up in hospital several times with broken bones and she had hit him as he slept with the hugest mallet, the kind you find at the fairground to test your strength by ringing the bell. In fact, I think it was stolen after a trip to the fair. He had been ill for days after that blow. He had stayed in bed, complaining about headaches and blurred vision, while my mother just chuckled to herself.

Not long after the stabbing, he moved out, for which I was truly pleased. He was a brutish bully when sober and ten times worse when drunk, or even worse, way too nice and loving. However, we were still subjected to vile scenes for several years to come, from both of them. Us kids were caught in the middle of their bitterness and often subjected to their games and were played as pawns in their continuous battle.

Heaven

The sweet respite had come, time with my nan and grandad. A time when I felt loved, cared for and more importantly safe. Even though I was over the moon to be spending time with these wonderful 'normal' people, I was always laden with guilt over leaving my sister, alone, without me for protection. Of course, my nan had offered to take her, but my mum wouldn't allow it. Even though us kids were a bit of a nuisance, she relied on my sister as a kind of crutch, or excuse, something or someone to lean on because my mother had so many insecurities and hang-ups. I only realise this now, as I look back and contemplate her actions.

I worried myself sick as to what I had left her to, but I needed this time to remember what it was like to be a child. I couldn't survive continually dealing with the madness of that house, day in day out, without these times to look forward to.

I was so super excited to be with my grandparents, to be away from home, to be able to eat good food and experience new places. It really was a fairytale adventure to me!

As soon as I entered my nanny's house, which wasn't far from where I lived, it always smelt like home; cooking smells lingered, sausage rolls, cheesecakes and other yummy delights that I couldn't wait to scoff. It was so lovely and warm, always warm and inviting. All my nan's paintings, books and trinkets were all around, it seemed that she enveloped me as I entered her home, I felt so safe!

It was a safe place!

I don't think there was any of my grandad's personality anywhere. Maybe in the shed. No, definitely in the shed!

"You want a cheese scone, my darling?" My kind nan reached into give me a big hug. We stay embraced for a while. It was one of my favourite places to be, in her home, in her arms.

"Yes please, Nanny, I would love one," I reply, smiling from ear to ear.

I don't think that I ever smiled at home and I don't remember my mum ever holding me. That saddens me, that I can't remember the last time that I was held by my own mum. What brings even more sadness is that as my mum was laying in hospital, as I held my own daughter in my arms at twenty-eight years old, I couldn't bring myself to hug her. It was the last time that I saw her alive. I should have hugged her, but I hadn't at that time been able to understand the complexities of life and motherhood.

My nan sat me down on the sofa, which was old and really quite ugly but I loved it – it was comfortable and it kind of held you, like a giant hand. She returned swiftly with a plate of deliciousness. Her homemade cheese scones, one of her specialties, chocolate fingers, yum yum and some crisps. There was a nice drink of pop to top it off. I really thought, "I'm in heaven!" I seriously wished I could live there all the time, not just because of the constant supply of goodies, but because my whole being seemed to change there. I became a child again, I became happy, interested in activities, whether it was painting, writing or helping my nan in her beloved gardens, whatever it was, I saw joy in it. I also got to watch 'crap' TV, which was what my mother called it. My grandad loved cartoons, so I got to sit and watch them with him. It's superb to watch a fully grown man laugh his socks off at *Tom and Jerry*! My nan adored movies, old movies, where all the women are always beautiful, able to sing and dance, and the lead man is the kind who always does the right thing, treating the women like queens.

I guess both activities are a form of escapism, maybe for all of us.

"Right, let's have this little snack and get ourselves off to bed, we have an early start tomorrow." Nanny gives me a little wink, a nod to grandad's driving, which was extremely safe but inevitably painfully slow. "Are you excited to go to the New Forest, Soph, and see all the ponies?"

"Oh, yes, I'm super excited, I haven't slept for days. I don't think I will sleep tonight!" I reply, deciding not to tell her about the nocturnal activities at my mum's home.

"Pops, your tea's here, come on, we need to get to bed," she shouts, but rather sweetly.

"Okay, I'm coming, my love," my gentle grandad replies; he really is the best man in the world.

My nan is scared to leave me sleeping downstairs, so as the house is a 100-year-old two-up, two-down, I get to sleep in the bathroom on a camp bed and my grandparents have a bucket in their bedroom for their emergencies. I don't mind at all. When I was younger, I would probably have gotten in with them, even though they lived in a bigger house then and I had my own bedroom. I always dreamt that I would be able to live with them one day. That was my only bitterness towards them, that they had decided to move to a smaller property, after my great-grandmother had died in the living room of gangrene. She was an extremely scary woman, super old-fashioned. In fact, for years I thought she was Queen Victoria. She could make the most hardened person crumble. My mum had great respect for her, I think that she reminded her of one of her own grandmothers.

I had been to the New Forest before with my grandparents. The great expanse of greenery filled me with joy and wonder. The horses roaming freely gave me hope that I could also be free, free from the bonds and environment that I found myself in as a child. The horses were fascinating. How did they get to the forest and how come they were still allowed to roam free? It was quite amazing to me and my nan just loved it. I think it was the Romany gypsy in her blood. They were very often menaces, though, blocking the road. I mean they just didn't move. We would have to go around them, off-road, which for my lovely poor-sighted grandad was always perilous.

"Aren't they pickles, love? So funny. Oh, do be careful, don't hit them. Look, move over more." Nan gave my grandad some gentle instruction, even though she had never been behind a steering wheel in her life.

My grandad could be nothing but careful as we were only travelling about 4mph, slow and steady was my granddad through and through. I, of course, didn't mind, though, as it was so much better than the haphazard chaos that I lived in.

We eventually arrived at our campsite, which really was just a field with an old fella sitting by the entrance gate letting us in.

"Down the bottom of the hill, that's the wash facilities. Pitch wherever you like, first come, first served here," the old man instructed, not really taking his eyes from the paper he was reading.

We spent the next half an hour checking out the site and finding the best place to pitch our tent for the next week. There wasn't much of the site, it was just a field with a very ugly toilet block on it. I was totally in love with the place, though, it was freedom for a week.

"Look, here's great. Let's put up the tent here."

"Ok, love, whatever makes you happy. Go and explore, Soph, while we pop up the tent." Grandad winked at me as he opened the boot of his beloved old blue car.

The tent was a big beautiful thing, I even had my own room. I found this amazing and we had all the mod cons: cupboards, cooker and a loo! It was a lovely little home. Erecting it all took some time, though, so from experience I knew that I had a few hours to kill. I had lots of time to go exploring the countryside or see if there were any kids my age to make friends with. I always made lots of friends while away on holiday. It felt nice, that no one knew who I really was or where I came from; I never ever mentioned my mother. This time I decided to sit on a fence gazing at the countryside and feel the sun get warmer as it crept higher in the sky. As far as the eye could see, there were fields or forests, with only a few houses dotted here and there; it looked lonely as well as peaceful, which made me shudder a little, as being alone made me feel so very vulnerable.

The campsite started to fill up slowly but surely, as more happy families arrived. Children began running around, screaming with excitement. Fathers and mothers making house. It was another reminder for me, how different my life was to other kids. As much as I adored my grandparents, and these holidays were a life saver for me, I still wished I had a 'normal' family and it was my own parents pitching a tent while lovingly smiling at each other.

"Hey, I'm Frankie, what are you doing there?" A pretty blonde girl in a pink flowery dress smiled at me.

"Hi, I'm just sitting and looking. I'm Sophie, want to explore?" With that, I jumped off the fence and my new friend and I went exploring for the next few hours, until I hear my name being called faintly in the distance.

"Soph, Soph, dear, come and get a drink and a bite," my nan calls, always thinking about everyone's needs and particularly their tummies.

The week whizzed by in a fun frenzy of exploring with my newfound friends and exploring in the car new places to visit, normally castles and gardens, which my nanny adored. I suppose most girls my age wouldn't be impressed by those kind of activities, but I was just over the moon to be out of the flat and going places. My favourite thing to do was always the beach, so on the days that we visited, I felt I had gone to heaven, the sand between my toes, the sound of the waves gently hitting the shore. There were always donkey rides and amusements to ignite the day with further thrills. Of course, there was plenty to eat as well; fish and chips for tea and throughout the day we would feast on my nan's picnic and ice cream. It was always on these days that I really wished that my sister could have been with us, to experience all this joy. The guilt and shame started to set in, and I would start to get a little sullen again, knowing that soon I would be back at home and my adventure would be over.

Usually we would bring along one of my new friends to the beach, which was great fun and a real privilege, however this just made me feel even more guilt, like I was replacing my sister and leaving her behind to deal with all the crap... like I was a deserter.

The sun always seemed to shine while we were on holiday and the innocence of the environment and people that I was around helped me feel like a child again, carefree and full of laughter. I always knew that it wasn't true, that I was living a lie, a feeling that haunted me, just there in the background, reminding me that I was a fake. Ah! That old friend, imposter syndrome. Yep, he became a close companion early on in my life.

These holidays were always fraught with a little childhood mischief. Like the time my cousin encouraged me to jump across a rather large stream, more like a river, to a cute little inviting island. I instead jumped right in the middle of the water and had to be rescued. Or the time my cousin and I helped a girl we had met and taken a dislike to jump right in the middle of quicksand; she also had to be rescued and we got into a lot of trouble. My cousin didn't holiday with us that often, though I would have like her to.

However, I didn't need another child to cause trouble, I was quite capable of doing that all by myself, and my nanny wasn't averse to a little bit of misbehaving. Like the time she led me across a field where there were some fierce-looking cattle. When we reached the middle of the very large field, the herd started to make their way towards us, and then my giggling nanny proceeded to declare, "Oh, they hate red, that's why they charge at the matadors, swinging red caps." There was a twinkle in her eyes. To which we both looked at my outfit in horror. Red, complete red, t-shirt, shorts and even red flipping shoes!

"Come on, we better run!" She pulled my hand and we started running, well more like running, skipping and tripping down holes. Of course, the herd started to move faster because we were interesting idiots moving like Quasimodo across their home. As we reached the safety of the gate – from certain death, I believe! – I turned around and the animals were just gazing at us in amazement; they really seemed to be perplexed by our behaviour.

"Bloody hell, that was close," Nan observed with a wink.

That sealed my fear of cattle.

The journey home to Kent was always a sombre one, for all of us. I think my grandparents didn't want me to return home either. I dreaded it because my mother would always make me pay for my week's desertion of them. She would be truly spiteful, and full of venom. The only gem of light was my little sis and the cuddles we enjoyed, and being able to protect her once more.

Even though I did feel so thankful to my grandparents for the joyful holiday, as they left me at the flat, I did feel resentment towards them for not taking me to their delightful home, full of love.

As expected, returning home was full of turmoil, even though I had hoped for the best, a miracle maybe, a sober mother and a home not filled with strangers that creeped me out. My sister and I were always joyous to be back together.

"Soph, I've missed you, tell me about your holiday," she nearly screamed as she ran towards me, jumping into my arms and giving me the biggest hug ever. It always felt good to see her and know that she was safe. She was the only pure thing in that place we called home.

As normal, my mother treated me with disdain, a traitor to the home, a deserter. How dare I enjoy myself and experience anything other than this life?

"Bit fatter, I see," she enjoys telling me. She had for several years been informing me of all my shortcomings.

"Oh, crazy girl" was a favourite followed by informing me I was fat, ugly and totally stupid and that so and so was this, that and the other and better than me in every way. I had become a girl who felt that I was lower than worthless, there was no purpose for me to be there, in fact I was just in the way. My father didn't want me, my mother hated me, it was just my grandparents that loved me and even they wouldn't take me from this place. I truly felt alone in the world and I would often pray that I would one day find out I in fact belonged to a loving family. *I just wanted to belong and be loved!* That's all any of us ever want, even as adults.

At least I had school to look forward to. School was my sanctuary from that place. I loved walking into school, smelling the school dinners cooking as I turned the corner of the building. I knew I was safe there. I loved the routine and total lack of chaos. I wasn't particularly bright, but I did enjoy learning and some subjects really captivated me, like history and art. However, I lacked confidence at school, and I felt beneath everyone in looks, intelligence and family background, so this held me back greatly and not just for my school years. No one told me I was good at anything or that I should follow my dreams. Surviving was all I could hope for. Council estate, pregnancy, and all those other lovely things that I was seeing daily. I always thought, privately, "No, I'm going to have a decent family life."

And, I did, I made a decision that I wouldn't fall victim to that way of life. My children, if I had any, would have a different childhood.

In Hiding Once Again

"I'm off out, don't know when I'll be back. He's coming, don't let him have her!" she orders me while pointing at my sister, who is sitting quietly looking at a book.

"What?! I can't stop him, don't go, or take her," I pleaded.

"Oh, don't be so selfish and stupid," my mother hissed back at me as she flounced out of the door.

As she left, my friend Fi arrived.

"Hi, all right, where's your mum off too? She looks nice."

I shrugged my shoulders. "Don't know and really don't care." My mood was already dark in anticipation of my step dad turning up.

"I have to look after my sister today, she can just come with us," I informed my friend, a little too snappy, really.

"That's okay, she's no problem at all. Shall we take a picnic to the park?" Fi tried to lighten the mood.

"I'm hungry, Soph. Where's mummy?" she whispered as she rubbed her tired eyes.

"I'll get you some toast... or something," I replied hopefully, as I headed towards the kitchen.

At that same moment, the front door shook with a bang. We all jumped in surprise and then stared at each other.

"Oh shit, it's him, shhhh." I turned round to the other two trailing behind me.

"What, who?" Fi asked, confused. While my scared sister just stared up at us both.

Another bang made us jump once more.

"Quick, in the bathroom!" I push them both to the bathroom, where we shut the door, crouch down by the toilet and hope he doesn't bash the door in. My friend and my sister don't really know what is going on or why we are hiding by the toilet. Though, of course, my sister recognises her father's voice, which is why she stared at me, waiting for me to give her answers.

"I know you're in there, open the fucking door, you bitches," he screamed as he banged the door with such force that I felt all the windows rattle. With that, I heard him trying windows in the flat and I just prayed that they were all shut. Thank God it was in the daytime because he would definitely have broken in if it wasn't for other people going about their business.

"Why are we hiding?" my sister whispered in my ear. "Is that my dad? He sounds cross and mean today."

"Mummy said you are not to go with him, I don't know why, I'm just doing as I'm told." I shrugged.

"I want to be with you anyway and he is scary sometimes." She started to cry.

With that there was a huge bang on the bathroom window.

"When I get hold of you bitches, I'm going to kill you. You dirty whores," he threatened as he continually banged the window.

"Please, shhhh. He'll be gone soon. Don't worry." I tried to comfort her in my most confident voice, while being as quiet as I could.

"Oh, my God, he's mad, there's no chance he can get in, is there?" Fi asked in a worried tone.

"No." At this point, I was so scared I actually could have wet myself, but I had to remain calm for those two, my poor little sister, who didn't deserve this first thing on a Saturday morning, and my friend who only came round to hang out.

With that it all went silent. We all looked hopeful at each other. The front gate swung shut, and we all breathed a sigh of relief.

We decided to stay where we were for a while just in case he was bluffing us and came back. After ten minutes of near silence and my sister nearly falling back to sleep, we all agreed that it was safe to move.

So, after giving my little sister some breakfast, we made a quick trip to the shop for a few little picnic goodies for a trip to the park. Luckily my mother had taught me how to shop without money as, of course, we had been left no money for goodies. We enjoyed a great day splashing around in the stream and enjoying the childish freedom of the park. The feeling of abandonment and terror subsided, if only for a short time, but we were thankful for the afternoon of childish fun.

She Left Us, Again

Sometimes, I yearned for my mother not to be around so much, as it was so much calmer without her there. There were no wasters or unsavoury characters around, and I didn't have to put up with her drunkenness and spitefulness towards me. However, her absence did make us vulnerable and I also wanted a mum. My young life and mind was full of constant confusion; unfortunately this is something that I carried into adulthood.

On this occasion, the three days' respite was welcome and enjoyable. She disappeared, which left me in charge, a young teenager in charge of a home and a little one. As strange as it sounds, this was my first thought: "A chance for a normal life!"

Even though my mum didn't announce that she wouldn't be back, I kind of guessed by the end of the first evening and day. So, instead of worrying or contacting anyone, though there wasn't really anyone to contact, I decided to make the best of the situation.

We did not have much food in the house, I needed to remedy that situation first, so out came the big snob bag and off to the shop I went, leaving my sister at home.

Luckily my mother had taught me a skill that I was extremely good at: *shopping!*

By this point, I had realised that I didn't have to rely on my mother or anyone to feed us, I had the power to do that, if not the cash. Of course, I did feel a lot of shame about it, however we needed food more than I cared about the shame. So off I went on my shopping trip.

"Just wait here, I'll be super quick and then we will have some lunch. Play with your dollies," I pleaded. I hated to leave her, I felt I was doing exactly what my mother was doing, however this was a necessary evil and I would only be fifteen minutes because getting caught wasn't an idea that entered my brain.

The bag that I used for my shopping trip was huge and empty. I slung it over my shoulder as I breezed into the store, with an air of confidence about me, trying to seem 'normal'. I was in the shop no longer than five minutes, my shopping trip was complete and we had all that we needed for the next few days. I felt a sense of relief in knowing that I could care for myself and my sister, even if it was in an extremely unconventional way. I had developed self-reliance and resilience at a very young age and I am so grateful that I did; both qualities have served me well throughout my life.

As I walked down the road carrying my bulging and extremely heavy bag, I smiled to myself, job well done, we would be fed and I was looking forward to the goodies I had picked up. The only problem with a teen doing the 'shopping': it wasn't a very well balanced haul. But at least we had food.

We spent a few days without any dramas or nastiness, which was great for my nerves. I felt happiness as well as achievement. From being made to feel useless to definitely being of great use gave me a little joy. I hated feeling as if I was nothing but a pain, useless and always in the way.

My mother turned up one morning after a few days. I watched her out of the window. She jumped out of a truck with some fella that looked like a cowboy. She was smiling, she looked refreshed and extremely happy after her break.

She waltzed into the flat without a care in the world.

"All right, Soph, all okay? This is Gary." She smiled at me. "Right, make yourself scarce." She ushered me out of the front room.

With that, I took myself off to the swings and sat looking at the flat, thinking how disappointed I was that she was home. I sat there finding it hard to comprehend how she could behave the way that she did! It seemed normal to her and the fact that I thought that our lives should be different… that made me the mad one! But I knew even as a small child that life could, should and would be different for me, some day!

She Found Some Happiness

For a time, my mother had a boyfriend who I thought was extremely nice. He was gentle in his voice, calm, terribly loving towards my mum and kind to us kids. He did look as if he had just stepped out of the 1960s, long hair, flares and waistcoat. He really rocked this style and his relaxed nature drew my mum to him. I think she may have been smitten.

He had a great big German Shepherd dog called Henry who was equally calm and nice, who we totally adored, and, as always showed us kindness, understood us and didn't want anything from us apart from love. Don't you just dig animals?!

This man was on the scene for a short while and it was very enjoyable. We didn't have all sorts calling on my mother, she didn't disappear and she seemed less nasty to me. She seemed happier and she was probably in love with him, hopeful for the future, maybe. I was certainly hopeful for a childhood that I saw portrayed on the TV or the kind of childhood that I knew my peers at school experienced.

Like most good things in my childhood, it didn't last for long. One morning he was there and the next he disappeared, never to be mentioned again. I was concerned as I didn't want things to return to normal, but they did with a huge bump and really, really quickly.

I was used to the police visiting my home. I was even used to our home being raided, but this raid was of gigantic proportion. Police cars and vans swooped down our road, the door was smashed in and there was no room to breathe in our flat as it was packed with police and dogs.

I was crying, my sister was crying and my mother was looking quite miffed. Apparently the calm and decent man who had shared our home for several months had attacked a police officer and they were searching for him. I think my mother was telling the truth when she said she had no idea where he was. The police still ransacked our home, I don't know where they thought he may be hiding in our tiny flat. Knicker drawer, perhaps?

The one thing that did irritate me was their dogs scaring my new ginger kitten that I had acquired. My love of animals and a need for their truly unfaltering loyalty is a continuing theme throughout my life. So, I told them in no uncertain terms that they were all mean for making children and a poor little kitten frightened. To which they grunted, then laughed and then completely ignored me. Another continuing pattern for a child like me, being ignored by those in authority.

We never did see my mum's lover again or hear what had happened to him. I don't know if my mother ever did but she never spoke of him. Henry the dog stayed for a little bit longer and we fell deeper in love with him. Then one morning we woke up and he was no longer around.

"Where's Henry?" I pleaded, not really wanting the answer as I started crying.

"Oh, he followed Sharon up the road last night and didn't come back." She shrugged.

My mum never looked for Henry, so we never saw or heard about him again either. Within a matter of weeks, both were no longer part of our lives, which was a shame as I felt safe with Henry around.

It seems that they departed as quickly as they came and I hated my mum for it. On reflection, I think my mother got rid of Henry because she couldn't afford to feed him. I often felt tremendous sadness about Henry's disappearance. I was learning as I grew that giving your love to someone, or something, is a tricky business because nothing good lasts long. I began to protect myself by not getting close to people and, in that way, I could protect myself.

Eye-Candy

It seems all mums like a little bit of eye candy once in a while and the mothers where I lived were no exception. The candy came in the form of Tom, who lived up the road from us. He was a wild free spirit who looked like he could play a toyboy to Alexis Carrington on Dynasty, normally clad in denim with a shock of blond crazy hair.

Even though he was easy on the eye and most of the local mums took a fancy to him, he was always causing some kind of trouble. From using an air gun to shoot near some mums enjoying a picnic on the green in front of our home to being the guy that everybody visited when they needed a certain 'pick-me-up'.

The trouble that he caused unknowingly for us occurred early one morning when we had a visit from a police officer who wanted to ask my mum some questions about Tom, which was unusual in itself, so I guess she owed the policeman a favour.

What I couldn't understand, until after, was why my mum was sweating like someone who had just run a marathon, while this man sat in a big old wooden chair that turned into a table, which my mother had acquired a few days earlier. She was clearly nervous and couldn't wait for him to leave.

I sat and watched for about an hour as she carefully answered all the questions, not giving too much away but enough for the policeman to be satisfied. He kept asking if she was all right, so he *had* noticed that she was not in a good place.

"I have a virus, it's really horrific, sickness and the shits, and it's catching," she informed him, intentionally not being at all subtle. He didn't take the bait, he obviously wasn't as stupid as she thought or hoped.

I actually enjoyed watching her sweat and panic. Sometimes I thought quietly to myself that she deserved everything that she got, for all the pain that she put us through.

Finally, he seemed satisfied with her answers and the relief on my mother's face was extremely visible. As he got to the door, he turned and looked straight at my mother. "I'll see you soon."

As she closed the door, she let out a huge sigh of relief before heading straight to the kitchen, finding her favourite green teacup and pouring herself some of her 'medicine'.

Later that day, the same policeman returned, to the utmost shock of my mother.

"That lovely seat in your front room," he began, "can I take a look at it?"

By this time in the day she was drunk, so a little cockier.

"Yeah, sure." She tottered down the hall.

"Where did you get this?" he ordered, with a knowing smile creeping across his face. He already knew the answer, without a doubt.

She stared blankly. She obviously hadn't got her story straight as his next words were: "I think you'd better come down to the station to answer a few questions."

My mother, knowing that she had no way to wheedle herself out of this, got her coat and left, no words to us.

It turned out that the beautiful chair belonged to a local monastery and was extremely ancient and incredibly valuable. It had appeared one night, mysteriously, and got taken away later that day. Maybe my mother should have sold it quicker.

Council Estate Stories

Listening to adults as a kid is always a dicey activity.

"So, she was just taken off the street? No one has any idea?" My mum's voice carried from the next room.

"Yeah, that's right, the police are looking for her," was the reply. I didn't recognise the voice.

"Well, that's weird in itself. On this estate, everyone knows everyone else's business! You can't do anything here and not have one person know the details," my mum scoffed.

It seemed one of the local kids, a girl called Faye, had disappeared off the street one day. All the adults seemed to be talking about it in hushed tones for several days and then suddenly the girl reappeared.

"What?! She was just dropped back? Where she was taken from? And no one knows anything?" my mother asked her friend as we stood outside the shop.

"Yeah, and the police are no longer involved apparently. It's crazy!" her friend added.

"Well, this is a very strange and crazy place!" my mother chuckled.

From this point, whenever I had to go out at night to run errands for my mum, she made me carry an open pepper pot in my pocket.

"If anyone tries to grab you, chuck that in their eyes and run!" she would offer.

Luckily I never had to use my deadly weapon while on my errands because I probably would have covered myself in it, being quite clumsy. And even if it met its target, I'm not sure it would have made any difference. I never felt vulnerable while on my mother's missions, I loved the dark and people seemed to look out for me, for the most part, anyway.

No one ever spoke of the girl that briefly disappeared again, not that I heard of anyway.

As I've grown older, I've often wondered about this event and the girl who was involved. What really did happen?

Ultimately, I counted my blessings that I wasn't that girl. Even with all the dramas and unpleasant events that I did encounter within my life, I still think, at least that didn't happen to me.

Angelic Visitors

Finding unusual objects and people was never a strange occurrence in the flat, there were always weird and interesting individuals floating around, along with mysterious objects arriving and disappearing. Nothing and no one really surprised me after a while.

However, that morning, as a sleepy teenager, I emerged from my bedroom, rubbing my eyes and hoping to return to bed but knowing that I couldn't. I was greeted by a large, beautiful life-sized white statue of a woman, half naked holding her own breasts. To say that I was dumbfounded was an understatement. I stood staring at the figure, rubbing my eyes, wondering if I was still dreaming. As my gaze moved down the hallway, I realised my new friend was not alone; the hallway was a party of half-clad statues with various bits of their private parts out. There must have been ten of them in the hallway. I was so shocked, because I had heard no noise the previous night, so it was as if the statues had just appeared by themselves.

For some reason, I decided to look in the living room. It was as if I already knew. Five women of white stone stared back at me, with their perfectly formed breasts and sweet but slightly demonic smiles. I was in some kind of nightmare and these things were going to come alive and kill me, surely. This was too much for my teenage hormones to bear, so off to the kitchen I went, squeezing by pointing stone fingers, flicking hair and nipples. Just then my mother wandered out of her room.

"Morning!" she said as she passed by me into the kitchen, in a pretty jovial mood.

I knew better than to ask, she would never tell me the truth anyway, and really, what did it matter to me? Our new guests were already here. I decided to take the happy mood stance instead.

"Morning, Mum. Tea?"

"No, thanks love, I already have a drink." She smiled back as she lifted her favourite green teacup to her lips, and sighed with relief as the contents went down.

I felt a pang of disappointment as I realised that it was only 7am and she was already drinking her 'medicine'. But, on the other hand, she hardly ever used any terms of endearment for me, so even though I knew by the time I returned from school she would be a different person, it felt nice for her to call me love, for now anyway.

"Okay, I'm going to get ready for school," I called as I disappeared back into my bedroom, trying not to get hooked onto a stone body part.

By the time I returned from school, all the figures had disappeared; vanished. It was just as strange walking into the flat and for them not to be there as it was waking up to them. There was a strange feel in the flat as well. I could smell cooking, and my mum was humming.

Now, not one to look a gift horse in the mouth, I took my mum's happiness and cooking and enjoyed them as if they were the finest chocolates in the world.

As an adult and a mum myself now, I realise that my mum no doubt really enjoyed those times of homely bliss as well. It was a magical experience that she had been chasing for most of her own life and never really got a chance to fully enjoy it. Just as it was in her grasp, it eluded her again and she fell back into the cycle of pain and self destruction.

Pretty Women in Canterbury

Shopping trips were always interesting with my mother. What teenager girl doesn't like to shop? This particular shopping trip was different from our normal trips out. For one, we went to Canterbury on the train rather than jumping on the bus to go into town. Secondly, my mother taught me a new way to shop, using a chequebook.

She had taught me how to sign the cheques the previous night. We spent hours making sure I had perfected the signature. On the morning of our little excursion she made sure that I dressed older than my teenage years before we headed out of the door. I was beyond excited as she said I could get some new clothes. Her little bribery worked well, as I played my part in her plans to perfection. For once, she had no complaints, and I was overjoyed that I had pleased her and she was happy.

We spent a whole day in Canterbury, in and out of fantastic stores. We had bags and bags, it felt like the scene out of *Pretty Woman* but instead of a man paying for it all, a stranger was, and they had no idea!

We went for lunch at Pizza Hut, where I filled up on everything possible and enjoyed not running out before paying, for once. I started to feel very grown up and I enjoyed not having to shoplift. I didn't realise at the time that what we actually were doing was a whole different ball game, a whole new league. Even if I did, I wouldn't have been able to refuse my mum, anyway.

Of course after a full day, we had to leave our role play to collect my sister from school.

"Not a bad work day at all," my cheery mum chirped as we jumped off the train.

My mother had loads of great designer goods that she could sell on and I had a couple of outfits that I could look cool in. *At last,* I thought. I felt that I always looked like a freak!

One outfit in particular that I was super proud of was a grey and red short dress, very 1980s and just right for a teenage girl. I enjoyed that dress for a couple of weeks before one day, after returning from school, I discovered my mum had sold it.

"We need to eat!" was her retort when I let her know how upset I was. My short period of looking nice was over. The payment for my dishonesty that day was gone, I just did what I was told, when I was told. That was expected of me and that's what I did at that time. I kept dreaming of a time that it would be different.

I was never fearful about the activities that I had to take part in. I was more fearful of my mother and I knew that was how we lived or we didn't live. I chose eating, wearing clothes and not waiting for someone to fix our problems. My mother helped me learn resilience and being self-sufficient. Yes there were better ways to learn it, but in my childhood that is what was needed to stay afloat, sane and in one piece.

A Night
on the Town

I started going to clubs with my mother at about thirteen-ish. Dressed up, I looked a hell of a lot older and everyone loved a young girl; well, men did anyway. My mother did start to get jealous. As her beauty faded, she seemed to enjoy making me feel pain by putting me down in some way. I've come to realise with age that this is an addict's trait, they love others' pain. It seems to detract from their own, even if it is only in a small way and momentarily.

Even though my mother was a raving drunk and enjoyed – well, maybe not enjoyed, needed – a man's company, she was always careful for me not to drink and to stay away from men. I was just the bait to hook the dozy, stupid fish.

This evening ended a lot differently to how it began and it's only as I look back, many years later, that I see things a little clearer. I realise and can admit to myself what happened and the magnitude of it.

This particular evening, I was allowed a drink. I always enjoyed dancing, so it was fun. I felt that I was bonding with my mum and the interest from men was a boost to my low self-esteem because, for the most part, I was told I was ugly, fat and unintelligent. Those words stuck to me like glue; I always believed that I was below others, that I should be grateful for any attention that I received.

One particular young man seemed to be showing me interest and for once my mum didn't seem to want to scare him off, which was beyond strange. I just decided she thought I was now grown up and this is what grown ups did: drank, danced and flirted. At this point I was loving life.

I don't know how the evening unfolded, all I know is that the next morning I awoke in this man's room with no recollection of the previous evening's ending. He took me outside to an awaiting taxi, told the taxi where I lived, kissed me sweetly and waved me off.

I was sure my mother was going to go crazy. However, as I walked in, still in shock from the bizarre beginning to the morning, she smiled sweetly.

"Morning, love. Okay?"

I said very little, as I felt so ill. I just went to my room and stayed there for the day. I pushed this episode clear from my mind as I didn't want to think about how strange it was, where I ended up, my mum's odd attitude to the events and the outcome of the evening and actually how I couldn't remember anything about the end of the night.

Another experience that made me feel low and disgusting for years, so I just tried to block it from my mind. I've realised now that I was still a child and adults took advantage; those that were there to protect me, didn't. I did nothing wrong or out of the ordinary for a teen, other than put trust in those that I shouldn't have.

Golden Joyride

Growing up, becoming a teen and growing into a young woman is an experience that is fraught with mistakes, wildness and hiding experiences from your parents, in most households.

My mother treated me as a child when it suited her, then on other occasions she would embrace my participation in activities that would shock most parents. One such time was when I was nearly sixteen. My mum had a boyfriend called Dick, another vile bully who liked to dominate women and girls in between drinking and fighting in the local pub, pretending he was a big prize fighter. This time he had been arrested, I expect for fighting, but for whatever reason he wasn't around.

Oh, the joy! I cherished every minute that was not filled with the dramas of my mother and her lovers or friends.

However, his pride and joy car, a gold Granada, sat outside, taunting my mother and, if I am honest, me. I really disliked this man. He was disgusting in so many ways!

Always one to rope others in on her little jaunts, she enlisted two willing teenagers: me and my boyfriend. We took the car on a joyride around our estate, which as sixteen-year-olds we found thrilling. But why a forty-something-year-old mother found joy in the experience, I don't know. I think it was probably because of all the trouble that could arise because of this little bit of fun we thought we were having.

Some people relish in others' misery or mistakes, and my mother was certainly one of those. She loved trouble of all kinds, as long as it was directed at someone else. If Dick found out, he would have become completely out of control on all of us. There is no doubt that one of us, if not all of us, would have been on the receiving end of that anger.

On top of that, if the police had caught us, we all would have been in trouble, including the boy driving, whose family would have been distraught. This would have brought my mother great joy.

For her, being in trouble with someone, even the police, was just a daily occurrence. I'm sure she enjoyed it because she didn't know what positive attention was. Any attention was better than no attention. She carried this from childhood, when no one wanted her; this led her from one shit relationship to another, from one mistake to another, increasing in severity as she travelled her path.

Unfortunately, my sister and I took a little of that as we went happily into adulthood believing our lives would improve, putting our happiness in the hands of others. I've learnt you can't make the right choices outside of yourself until you deal with what is going on inside of you and realise how bloody amazing you really are.

By all accounts I shouldn't be here, but I am and I AM ENOUGH!

There Goes the Salad

Back in the distant life of my childhood, all things, people and behaviours seemed to have been alien, not real and very surreal. For a long while, I believed that I was remembering them wrong, that they were jumbled in my frazzled mind, but I now know that they were not, and are not.

That life seems like it was lived by someone else, in another time and I am just watching it unfold on my internal movie screen. My morals, beliefs and ways to stay alive were so different to how I now live. My mum did what she had learnt throughout her tough and lonely life and she struggled to live by a standard set by society.

One such time was when my mum and stepfather were invited to a BBQ by some nice folks in the estate that joined onto ours. My mother even made a rice salad to take along; she was an amazing cook when she put her mind to it.

She had decided that she would drive my stepfather's Triumph, which was a lovely little car. This isn't strange in itself until you add the fact that she hadn't driven for years, and I mean years. In fact, I don't believe that she even owned a valid licence, ever.

My mother was always extremely impatient, and added to already being drunk before leaving the house, she decided not to wait for him as he finished getting ready or drunk, I can't remember which.

She set off merrily, with little Jemma in a carrycot, laid across the back seats – before the times of safety belts in the back – and her precious salad strapped in the front seat. It seems that she crashed John's beloved car just outside of the BBQ venue sending the carrycot and Jemma flying forward and my mother saving the salad. No one seemed to be hurt from the minor setback, and my mum, Jemma and the salad carried onto the party, leaving the sad little car to be dealt with at a later date.

Nothing stopped an afternoon of frolicking in my mum's life, it was fun and games the whole way, for her. I guess that's how she forgot how sad she actually was.

She Flew Through the Door

My mum used to seem to want to make me feel bad, particularly as I became a teenager. I don't know if it was intentional or she just felt bad herself. Or, maybe she was just trying to make sure that I didn't make the same mistakes that she did. I will never know the answer to that, but I like to think that she wanted more for me and that was one of her crazy-arse ways to protect me.

One particular occasion was when she wouldn't let me go to the local youth club. There was no reason why I was not allowed to go, not a clear reason anyway. Most things, reasons, experiences or even days were not clear back then! It was a time of constant confusion. I hate any kind of confusion now, but I have learnt it's one of the techniques addicts use to hide the real stuff that needs dealing with.

So, trying to be rebellious, I decided to climb out of my bedroom window and go. I wanted to spend time with my friends, doing what teenagers did, laugh, talk about boys, eat goodies, roller-skate (it was the eighties), and generally, for me, just be a kid.

Well, I wasn't there long, enjoying myself and feeling a little smug that I had got one over on her. By this time I hated her, I didn't understand her pain, I only understood mine. Well, as she flung herself through the glass doors to this safe haven for kids, run by happy, loving volunteers, my heart sank. My face dropped, I went green and I hoped the ground would just swallow me up. Surely that would be the kind thing to do.

"Oh God!" In my head, I prayed for some kind of intervention.

It didn't come.

"Oi, you, you little shit, what do you think you are doing?"

The whole place went quiet. My friends that knew my mum looked at me in sheer pity, but those that didn't know her were looking at each other and the leaders in total shock and bewilderment, no doubt thinking, "Who's this woman?!"

The adult leaders just stood frozen, looking at the scene that unfolded in front of them at lightning speed.

She was clearly drunk; no change there, then. She marched towards me like a soldier marching to battle. As she did, everyone around me stepped back, but I stood dead still, still in disbelief that this scene in the film that was my life, was playing out in front of all to see. I heard someone gasp behind me, then there was a snigger and then the giggling began.

"I told you to stay inside, now get the fuck home." She reached for my hair and grabbed me by it, dragging me out of the door with such gusto that I thought my hair may just rip off. I said nothing because I knew it would make no difference, and by that age I had decided showing my true feelings was a pointless act – a trait that I carried with me for years until I learnt how to truly express my feelings to myself firstly and then to other human beings.

Luckily, our home was only a minute away from the youth club but in full view of it. Just to add to my teenage humiliation, the entire club came outside and watched me be dragged home by the same piece of hair that she refused to let go of.

Not one person stepped in, not one adult told her to stop. This seemed to be the case my whole childhood, but even though it wasn't a million years ago, that was the way back then; even the authorities didn't step in until it was the very last option.

As she slammed the door behind us and turned to me, with a look of complete victory, evil victory, she spat out, "You will think fucking twice before doing that again, won't you?" She laughed as she turned away from me, knowing she had made me – a totally uncool, unattractive teen outsider – the laughing stock of the teens of the local neighbourhood.

I dragged my throbbing head and broken spirit off to bed. I knew when I was beaten. One thing that having my mum as a mum taught me was resilience and bouncing back. There's always a comeback. It's a true saying, "What doesn't kill you, makes you stronger", but I would add to that: "If YOU let it".

What was I going to do, sit in my room till I died? No, I had to go to school, go outside, go on my mum's errands. So, I would have to put up with the jeers, laughter and feeling like the village idiot. It wasn't the first time, it certainly wouldn't be the last and it was nowhere near the worst.

I now thank my mum for that resilience. Because of her, I had to develop a way to bounce back. I didn't know it had a name back then, I had never heard of the word resilience. But throughout my life, each time I fall, I may stay down a while, I may wallow in self-pity for a while, but I always know I must get up. That there is a way out. That it's my choice if I stay down or not because if a small child can bounce back then a fully grown woman can.

As if the embarrassment of being humiliated once again by my mother wasn't enough punishment, she decided to use the man she hated above all other men, my aggressive stepfather who no longer lived with us, to punish me further, as if I were some kind of total rebel living in a middle-class family, with parents who sat round the dinner table each evening and read to us at bedtime.

As much as my mother detested that man who once lived with us – and he had as much contempt for her, I guess he liked to play the big man and he enjoyed intimidating women – she told him of my horrendous crime and he decided to punish me too. But, because he liked to play with his prey, like some evil villain from a movie, I was given an option. "So, I'll give you a choice of punishments, as you are now becoming a young lady and should be in control a little," he said with a sly smile, enjoying every moment but trying to make out he was doing me a favour. "You can be grounded for two weeks or smacked," he said with a grin resembling a snotty-nosed bully boy after squashing a tiny ant.

Without batting an eyelid, I replied, "Smack."

With a shocked face, he questioned me. I knew he was trying to break me "Are you sure?"

"Yep," with defiance in my voice but not meeting his gaze.

Without knowing, my mum had taught me not to show fear in the face of danger or a threat and to always stand up for myself.

"Okay, you asked for it, I tried to give you the soft option." He tried to sound disappointed.

Soft option? Staying in that house for two whole weeks, I would go mad for sure. I loved secondary school, which all my friends found crazy. It got me out of the house, around 'normal folks'. Years later, I found out *normal* is overrated and really there is no *normal*. And I certainly now want to be anything but *normal*.

He sat down in the chair, took off his trainer and motioned for me to go over his knee, like a scene from *Just William*. However I was a teenage girl, so try imagining that.

He gave me three hard slaps with his size eleven white trainer, each one with more anger than the last. Though I winced with the intense pain, I would not shed a tear, not in front of him anyway. I refused to give him any more satisfaction than he now had. It angered him that I didn't cry. A little thin waif took back some of his power. The only control he could have over people, particularly women and girls, was to bully them.

He could try all he liked, I would not let him get to me. This ran continually through my head that day.

"It's for your own good, you can't sneak out at night." He reached over and tried to tenderly touch my arm as I disembarked from his lap. I hastily retreated to my room, not answering or engaging in eye contact.

My mum had been at the door the whole time, earwigging with glee. She was losing her grip on me as I grew, she knew it and it pained her.

I now realise that it wasn't only for selfish reasons, it was because she couldn't cope with loss, particularly of another child. She didn't realise that it was just a child growing up, that's what happens. As a teenager, I thought she was jealous, or worse just hated me, but she didn't want to lose another child; it didn't matter that she couldn't show me love. She wanted me close and wanted to control me, as she couldn't keep her first child close. He had been taken away from her when she was just a child herself.

I didn't engage with her either that day, but to be fair I hadn't for years and wouldn't really ever communicate deeply with my mother again.

No Home

Another time when my stepfather decided to side with and support my mother occurred around the same time. He wanted to play the 'man', the father figure of the household, even though he didn't live there and had already caused so much damage to all of us females in the home. Maybe he wanted to come back, who knows, but heavens be praised that he didn't.

This particular time, I must admit that my biological father and I were to blame, somewhat. I had watched my father and his new family live a beautiful, normal family life for years; watching from the side lines, there was no place for me in that idyllic setting. It affected me greatly at the time, to realise that I wasn't loved or valued by my very own father. He wouldn't have even seen me, if it wasn't for my grandma being a stubborn woman and taking me to see him every week! Bless her, she was a force to be reckoned with. She was an old-fashioned soul, who adored all her relations. She believed in family, coming from a large clan and a time when families used to choose to live close together. In her mind, she was doing her duty as matriarch, making sure her only son played his role as my father. Little did she know that it knocked my self-esteem so much, always feeling like the poor relation, unwanted, unloved and just a little snotty-nosed annoyance. I took these feelings into adulthood, always feeling lower than others, just the council estate kid, whose mother went to prison, trying to hide from the truth and certainly not letting others know my history.

Now I shout, hell yes, I am the council estate kid, with a drunk for a mother and look, I've survived and thrived... so can you!

So, can you imagine my delight as a teenage girl who, at the time, adored her father. I thought the sun shined out of his behind and I yearned for his love, his approval. My joy was complete after spending months dreaming of living with him in a home filled with love, calmness and happiness, where there was always food to eat, where adults didn't come and go, where I could act my age and be a child. My heart burst with complete contentment when, after spending a great deal of time plucking up the courage to ask whether I could move in, he agreed.

We had all been sitting in the front room on one of our family visits. My dad was laying on the floor, looking at the telly. He had been playing a game with one of my half-brothers, who had been taken up to bed. I could hear them running amuck above us. It was just us left in the front room; this was my moment.

"Dad, can I come live here?" I blurted out, so quickly I didn't even form the words correctly.

Without even turning his head to look at me he said, "Yeah, sure."

Looking back with hindsight on the year that I spent living there and the years that followed, he didn't want or need me there. The year there just reinforced my feelings that I had about myself and I was totally unhappy. After a year of knowing I was unwanted, I went back to my mum and a home that no child should live in.

I should have realised before I even moved in that I wasn't going to find the peace that I had always yearned for. Now, with my adult mind as I look back, it seems that we were always chasing peace, my mum, my dad and me. I don't think that my mum or dad ever found the peace that they were searching for... have I? I truly think that I have.

With the excitement of my news that I was going to live in a proper family, I skipped into the flat, full of joy and, of course, this set my mother off, so when I practically sang that I was moving out, she decided that she would help me on my way. Not in the way that I had hoped for either, but why would she be happy in losing another child?

Yet again, my stepfather stepped in to do her dirty work. He dumped all of my belongings on my dad's doorstep.

"Her mother said she's all yours." He turned his head towards me trailing behind him.

I was shocked but not worried because I was going to live with *The Waltons*! Or so I thought.

My father was shocked, but he wasn't as shocked as my stepmother, the woman who made it very plain to see that I was stepping on her toes. Even years before she had let me know that I wasn't welcome.

On family visits that were instigated by my nanny, the simple act of teatime let me know that I was an annoyance. I thought that she would grow to love me and treat me as her own. I was greatly mistaken; from the get-go, it was plain that I had upset the apple cart.

My father's and his wife's reply to my mother was to contact social services and say that they couldn't keep me. I remember a meeting at the social services offices. We all sat around a large table with lots of officials, discussing my future, without me saying a word. My mother didn't speak to me, she was hurt and betrayed, and I can now understand how she felt. My father and his wife just spent the whole time arguing strongly for my return to my mother, who made it very clear I was not welcome back there. The mood of the room was one of anger and upset, both parties wanting nothing to do with me and the officials just wanting the matter settled so they could leave the room. I sat listening to everyone's opinions of the matter and of me. My eyes went from one side to the other, listening, taking it all in and feeling the disdain of all those involved. No one seemed to realise that I was even there; maybe I wasn't meant to be, who knows. I wished I wasn't.

Anyway, that started the year of learning how unloved and unwanted I was. Yes, I was fed every evening, a proper dinner, which I truly relished, and I lived in a home where I was safe, but while their children were loved, praised and spoilt, I was just a pimple on their perfect lives.

I even stole my school uniform that year because buying me anything was a major drama. In that whole year living there, they bought me – a growing teenager – a pair of school shoes and a pair of trainers, which were so ugly and uncool but they wanted me to wear them to and from school, so I didn't wear out my school shoes. Just what a teenager who feels ugly, different and totally uncool needs, a pair of trainers that my nan would have worn. Needless to say, I wore said trainers only in view of the house and changed as soon as I could.

Eventually, my mother started to forgive me, and I started to visit her and my little sister, who I missed so much, it was as if a part of me was missing. I missed the love and cuddles that we shared, the connection and bond that developed through the sadness of our home. I didn't have this connection with my brothers, even though I hoped for it, they lived a different life and only had their childhood and childish things on their minds.

So, when I asked if I could come home, my mum shrugged and acted as if it meant nothing to her but still agreed for me to return. I jumped at it.

"Oh, if you must, I suppose. Jem probably will be pleased. Didn't think you would stick it with that horse-faced bitch this long," she laughed.

It was a small victory for her, in her eyes anyway, that I returned home.

It's funny that at the beginning both parties were upset and didn't want me and the year ended with them both ecstatic that I had returned to my original dwelling. My mother, of course, could not show her joy of my return, but my father's wife certainly made it known. It's strange because I thought she would enjoy the chance to be a mother to a daughter again, as her first daughter lived away from her. My dad was happy that there was peace once more in his home. Unfortunately, the contentment in their home didn't last for that long either.

I went home and realised that nothing had changed. In fact, things had been ramped up considerably. More drink, drugs, crime, men and sadness. I held shame for a long while that I had been a selfish teenager and jumped ship, leaving my sister for a superficial life that I thought would be better; served me right that it wasn't.

I was back and I would try to do my best for her from that moment on… I of course got it wrong on so many more occasions.

The Art of Scrumping

One of the fun, childish and innocent memories that I have, that I relish, that fills my heart with joy and puts a huge grin on my face, is scrumping... yes, you read that right, scrumping. I don't think kids today would know what that even is or that you could get into trouble for it. Yes, taking apples, beans, berries from someone's field or garden is a crime.

Even though our home was the normal bog-standard council maisonette, luckily it was built at the end of the war when the authorities, those in power, realised how important having a good-sized garden was for our health. So not only was the flat a really great size, the gardens front and back were huge, which meant that all our lovely elderly neighbours, who had experienced shortages during the war, dedicated part of their gardens to growing an assortment of delicious temptations for us hungry little terrors to pinch when no one was around.

For most kids, nicking an apple from someone's garden was just a little bit of pushing the boundaries, being naughty or just seeing what they could get away with. For me, sometimes, it was literally filling a hole, the hole in my stomach. When the local gardens were bursting with life, I could always nip here or there and grab something. What made my escapade easy was that all the gardens were joined in our road and the road that backed onto ours, just separated by the standard council shaky fence that could hardly hold back the local dogs.

I would flit from garden to garden, filling my tummy, imagining I was on some adventure in some far-flung place, living off my wits and what the earth could give me, my little mind full of adventures and fun.

One elderly neighbour called Mary was sometimes known to partake in a sherry or two with my mum, but on other occasions would let it be known very vocally that my mother and us kids were misfits of society. Anyway, Mary had some lovely trees at the bottom of her garden that were overgrown, twisted and knotted together. It was a place where I could hide and no one ever thought of looking there. I could daydream about my future life, about the family who had mistakenly given me up for adoption and would one day find me. I could savour my loot, which no one could take off me, and just be a child, with no one trying to make me do something. I could just be a little girl, a rascal.

Mary had a big white poodle dog, which hated children, so whenever it came into the garden I hid deeper and higher in the tree den. The dog would yap and bark at the tree, sensing an intruder but its master, who funnily enough had the same tight white curled hair, would usher it back indoors.

I loved my secret place and sometimes I could hear my mum shouting for me, no doubt to send me for her 'medicine' or fags. But, even though I knew there would be a price to pay when I went in, I enjoyed my solitude, munching the neighbour's homegrown foods.

I don't think I have ever tasted strawberries like the ones I borrowed from a local garden, or apples straight from the tree. The best, though, were runner beans straight from the garden; the joy of that crunch. The thing that I probably could have done without eating was the fruit from our own garden, rhubarb. Yep, I used to take great big stalks of it and munch it raw. I loved it! Well, I thought that I did because I ate copious amounts of it and I don't remember it having an adverse effect on me either.

I do remember that when my stepfather still lived with us he decided to give the neighbours a run for their money and have the best veggie patch, *ever*. Well, instead of starting small, he turned most of the garden into a mud pit, leaving us kids nowhere to play other than in all the muddy puddles, which we actually loved.

However, we didn't have a wondrous crop of different veg and fruits to fill our bellies. Instead, we had rows and rows of flipping cabbages and let me tell you there are only so many cabbages one family can eat. Surely even the Bucket family, in Charlie and the Chocolate Factory, had a limit. I know one thing, that I hated cabbages for years because of the number we had eaten during that period.

The novelty of growing food to eat didn't last long and soon the garden was returned to a jungle we could play in, but now it seemed to be filled with little hills and troughs where the cabbages had once lived.

Twinkle by Name and Nature

I always loved animals, I think because I could talk to them, share my secrets, rely on them. My nan and grandad didn't know half of what went on at home, so having someone, or something to talk to was so important. When my sister came along, at least I had an alliance, a buddy who I could bond with. But before that it was the most loyal and beautiful cat called Twinkle.

Twinkle was a black and white cat that my mum had adopted years earlier. Twinkle was my constant companion as I grew, snuggling me and comforting me with her sweet love. The sight of her beautiful face was enough to lift my mood. She had a little triangle of white by the side of her nose and the most luscious whiskers. It's funny, I have no pictures of her, but I can see her face as if I held her yesterday, nearly forty years on. She was such a sweet confidante. When I hold my cats now, it's as if I'm hugging her and saying thank you and sorry at the same time. You see, I feel that I let her down. I couldn't save her after all that she did for me, and I hadn't realised how much I still hurt and felt guilty about it, until this very moment, as I write this and the tears roll down my cheeks.

I didn't cause her any harm or neglect her. I just didn't realise how evil others were in my house and didn't protect her from that. My stepfather was cruel to the core. He disliked animals and they didn't enjoy being in his presence either. Dogs would normally growl or cower, and cats would disappear, as did Twinkle. She avoided him like the plague. It's just a shame that she didn't survive just a little longer, till he moved out.

I always had my suspicions as to why she died, but the truth only came to light years later, when his new partner made a joke of it. It was the last time that my family and I saw him. Some things are just unforgivable and, for me, this cruel act was it for me.

It seems that on an extremely cold December night he locked her out of the house and, because she spent every evening indoors, she didn't know what to do other than curl up by the back door. That is where my mum found her the next morning, frozen to death. I was about eleven and my best friend had gone. My mum hid the death from me until I returned from my grandparents' that evening by covering the lifeless creature with a blanket and burying her while I was out.

No doubt the cruel act was actioned while John was drunk and for some 'crime' that my mother or me had committed, which he obviously still found funny and was proud to share twenty-odd years later.

Apparently, if you don't come to terms with a situation, for instance a death, every time a new trauma occurs you relive that same event and grieve. I can relate to that because each time a family animal dies, my grief is all consuming. I never really understood this until I started to look at myself, my past and why I act a certain way. Sitting here thinking about my friend and the way she passed fills me with such despair, dread and disgust that I feel like that child again who wept uncontrollably for days and days, and no one hugged me as I mourned the loss of my friend.

As any child from an abusive home knows, when you find loyalty and devotion, you hang onto it, it's the core of survival. I was like that as a child and I still believe that true loyalty is so important in all relationships.

From that point, animals came and went from our home and I got attached to every one but, of course, none have ever replaced Twinkle. At one point, we had a Canada goose, which no doubt had been stolen or liberated. We called it Donald. I have no idea if it was a girl or boy, but I do know I loved it and it was fun to be around. It sounds bizarre as I write that, 'A goose was fun to be around'. Either the animal was strange, or I was. Maybe both!

Without doubt, it caused a stir with all the old folk of our road. A huge noisy and very vicious goose waddling around our council garden, hissing at everyone who dared to pass. My mother, who liked to stand out and play up to others' opinion of her, of course played up to this, inviting customers of the local pub to come and take a look at the poor beast who probably just wanted a quiet pond to swim across, which we didn't have.

As normal, after getting attached to Donald, he was gone in the blink of an eye. My mother awoke one morning to the garden covered in his feathers; apparently a fox had feasted upon him.

I expect that he was headed for someone's table come Christmas, anyway. If he was sold by the pound, he would have fetched my mum a fair bit of 'medicine' money and, for my mum, everything had a price on its head. So, either the foxes beat my mum to it and she lost a fair bit of money, or she got an offer that she couldn't refuse.

Unfortunately for Donald, he would have looked great on some stately home's dining table, so he was never destined to be my friend for long. I never knew where Donald came from or where he went, that really sums up a great deal of my childhood.

For a brief while, we had a dog called Daisy when I was about fifteen. I had come by her one evening on my travels. She was a puppy that no one wanted, and my mum had said we could keep her, if I helped provide for her, which of course I did. Borrowing a can of Chappie from the local Spar was not a problem. I even got some money together for her injections, which I gladly handed over to my mum as I thought she would take her to the vet and get her protected.

However, several months later, it became evident as we watched her die that my mum had decided against using the money for its intended reason. I found it terrifying watching this once feisty dog, who happened to go for my stepfather each time she saw him, dying from that dreadful preventable disease.

I must admit that the hate that I had started to feel for my mother began to run deep and she was just giving me more reasons to want to get away from her, forever.

OCD Starts to Hang Around

We all, well nearly all, suffer obsessions of some sort, if we are honest. Obsessive fears and addictive behaviours control some part of our being and lives. It could be drink, drugs, cleaning, a man, or exercise - I'm sure that the list could go on and on.

Well for a long period of my life I was obsessed with HIV, or at least not having it or catching it. This sounds as crazy as it really is, but it's true!

I worried 24/7 about it and was ignorant for years and years about how it was transmitted. Put it this way, I didn't use public toilets, for years and years!

Sharing a drink or food was yuk for me. Even kissing and hugging set me off. So, after sex, even with a long-term lover, I would spend hours in the shower cleaning myself outwardly and inwardly. It hurt physically and mentally; I was tired of the ritual of cleaning myself and my home. And did it ever really banish what I thought I was harbouring? I thought it was a disease but maybe it was just shame, guilt and dirt from the past that I needed to cleanse myself from. Was it that that was eating me away?

This weird and tiring obsession with this sad disease started in my early teenage years, where most irrational thought processes do.

My mum made friends with a kind, calm and caring man. He was to us, anyway. He lived with us for a spell and I never really knew why. I don't believe that he and my mother were romantically involved. I was under the impression that he had fallen on hard times and my mum felt compassion for him. He was considerably younger than her, so maybe she saw him as a son, the son that she lost.

He had AIDs. It was the eighties, the time when this illness was just surfacing. When AIDs started coming to the forefront of our minds, I didn't really understand anything more than the sensational headlines and panic. As a teenager who couldn't read very well, I never investigated further. I just knew that my mother's new friend, who shared our home, our bathroom, food, cups, plates, towels… actually everything, had this disease! For a child without all the information, the facts, the knowledge that I needed, all I could do was draw on my own childish, stunted feelings, beliefs and conclusions.

This lasted for years. Those beliefs and feelings that really should have been left in my childhood. For many years, even until my last pregnancy, I had a totally unhealthy worry about hiding this disease inside of me. I thought it laid dormant in me, waiting to strike at the most hideous moment, like the happy birth of my much desired baby, even though I knew this was not the case.

For years I had worried that if I had not caught the condition as a child, that I certainly would contract it as a grow up. I suppose for some stupid reason I thought that I deserved it because of conditioning as a child. I would spend nearly every waking hour worried about something. I wouldn't use any toilet but my own, unless I really had to. I would never share drinks, food or cutlery, even with people that I was close to. My mind and time was consumed with another skeleton that I had dragged around on my back. It was so tiring and so unnecessary.

I think of my mum's friend often and realise that he must have also lived in fear until the end of his life. That for him, back then, it was just a waiting game. He had no choice but to take each day exactly as it arrived.

Norfolk - A Mixed Bag

Even though I was not protected by the person who should have loved me, directed me and helped me fulfil my potential, some times were delightful and the sun shone upon me often, in my eyes anyway.

Not only time spent at my grandparents' was a delicious pleasure but also time spent in Norfolk, in the heart of the countryside, where I truly could run free. I loved it!

We spent a lot of time in Norfolk because that is where my stepfather came from and his family still lived there. His mother had a large, quite strange farmhouse down an old dirt track, with the nearest neighbours a good ten minutes' drive away.

This place offered freedom, room to breathe, think and be a child. As the majority of the adults were always in some stage of inebriation, the children of the large family were left to their own devices. This for me was sheer delight. We would play hide and seek in the corn field behind the house, we would run wild screaming, laughing and I would feel like a child. Kind of like Tom Sawyer, playing in streams, fields and climbing in trees, which I inevitably fell out of.

The house in itself was intriguing, stairs and corridors all over the place. Places to explore and hide in. A beautiful swirling staircase that of course the children enjoyed sliding down. I loved that house and still think of it often. My lovely little sister was actually born there one winter's night after all (yes all, even my mum) had got drunk. The birth even got into the local paper, I think because she was the first baby born in the house for 200 years, or something like that. Headline news!

There were some sad memories from the time spent there. Like when the dog had puppies. Us kids were all delighted but the last we saw of them was them being carried off by someone in the family, just a few days old. Another time involved a different family dog, who was called Bear. He disappeared while wandering around the local countryside, never to return. I found out later that he was probably shot by a local farmer. Of course, as a highly sensitive child, I was deeply upset by this fact and the fact that the adults didn't seem shocked or upset. But then dogs, cats, etc. were just commodities.

The Lion Cub

One person that my mum did speak about often with love, kindness and real dedication was James. I don't really remember James, only as some celestial being, he was there but not. I remember being part of the stories that my mother told and the feel of the stories, but I don't really remember the stories, detail by detail, just a ghostly outline of a dream.

My mum always collected an eclectic array of people around her. We had real hard-nosed 'proper' criminals, police, colourful artists and people that really shouldn't be in that kind of environment. So, James was just part of a cast of characters that passed through the show that was my mother's life.

I remember James like some biblical dream. He had dark, curly hair, was thin and flamboyant… and of course the lion! For me, at the time and always afterwards, it was a beautiful golden, purring kitten.

However, in reality it was a lion, a cub that had been purchased – I believe from Harrods – that's how the story went. James was apparently a fantastic hairdresser in London somewhere and I suspect my mum knew him before she left the city. It seems he had a great deal of wealth, but unfortunately, he also had a drug habit that made him end his days in Liverpool Street Station, giving his last breath to heroin.

When my mum reminisced about this man and his pet, I felt my part in the story, as a small child. I felt I was there, alongside her.

I don't know the story behind my mum and James departing or his departing from this planet. I know my mum was sad and always spoke highly and beautifully of him and the lion that had to be sold when it grew.

She was certainly consumed with grief about the departing of a dear friend.

I remember James and the lion and that brings warmth to my heart, as strange as that may seem. That was our life. Strange! Fleeting moments of strangeness!

Mum's Friends...
Or Were They Foes?

The collection of people that my mum knew was quite outstanding and it's a shame that she didn't use her obvious vivacious personality to attract people who would bring out the best in her. Instead, they all seemed to feed into the destructive side of her and the band of misfits grew each time she went on 'holiday'. She stayed in an array of prisons, some pretty tough ones as well, where she befriended a mixture of women, from women who would or had killed their own fathers to ladies caught stealing from the family company pension fund.

She mixed with them all and never seemed to encounter anyone's wrath. She pleased everyone and I remember letters that she received when she came home, thanking her for helping others while inside.

These friends never seemed to make up for what she was really yearning for. Looking back, with more knowledge on my side, I know that she was yearning for her son, taken by the authorities in 1962 with the help of her stepfather, her mother had already passed away or was in a mental institution, as she was also a drunk. It seems that the vicious cycle of not helping and punishing women, particularly those from lower classes, was still strongly evident in the 60s and affected us later generations of women. It certainly had a huge bearing on generations of women in my family.

My mother was also in need of her own mother and her siblings, of which there are a few scattered around, and it seems more sad stories reside there.

Being included, wanted and protected by your nearest and dearest, your blood, your childhood carers, is what most women desire, particularly when times are tough. And it seems that she never received that, either. She carried on down that vicious path with her own children.

She never met her son again and she kept him a secret all her life. She also never saw her family again and I believe the last time that she did was in the early sixties. She filled her life and our home with oddballs, misfits and craziness because she couldn't stand being on her own, even if it was just dragging her children around with her. We missed so much school because she couldn't go out on her own. Her childhood and early adulthood were taken from her along with those she loved, and she never recovered. Not only did she pay the price but us two girls did as well and her son, my lovely brother that I met a few years ago.

Loneliness was one of her biggest fears, being alone with her own thoughts and deeds.

Crawling Up
the Avenue

During the course of my life, you would think that after everything that I saw as a youngster, I would have steered clear of all the elements that caused our family so much pain and damage.

That wasn't the case, though I always knew that I would not emulate my mother's behaviour. I still had to learn for myself and feel the pain of bad choices as I matured – and boy did I learn – oh, and I still am learning. I seem to keep reliving the same mistakes. That saying, "You keep reliving the same drama, until you learn the lesson" is so true. So, please learn that lesson the first time and save yourself so much pain! It seems that I am a slow, very slow learner!

One such time was as a young teenager when I decided to find out what all the fuss was about alcohol was – why did my mum love it so much? Why was it her most important ritual? Why did it come before us?

So, in true teenager style, while hanging out with my friends in a local shopping centre, which we had just started to do, trying to catch the attention of the local group of hot boys, which I think we did but for all the wrong reasons, we decided that we wanted to look cool and hip. The only way to do that, we thought, was to have a drink. So, we decided to start off our drinking experience with something really classy… Scotch! What could possibly go wrong?

Of course, I 'borrowed' said alcohol from the shop. We laughed as we consumed the large bottle in the stairwell of the shopping centre, getting more animated as the afternoon went. We went from feeling cool, elegant and grown up to becoming sweaty tramps as we made our way home. I was found crawling along the road by a friend of my mum's.

The strange outcome of the episode, as well as me never touching Scotch again and my knowing that being a drunk wasn't for me, was that my mum went completely nuts at me. Hitting me full force with the angry, concerned parent, extremely disappointed with a rebellious teenager.

For all the things that she could have shown disappointment in over the course of the years, she picked this.

I was stunned as she was always drunk and I was just following in her footsteps, but she didn't want that, she didn't want her daughters to struggle with the dark demons that consumed her. She wanted us girls to be more than she had managed because she knew that her wonderful talents, energy and intelligence had been wasted.

I know that she wanted us to break that cycle and be more, have more and not follow her unhappy path. The only problem was that she was unsure how to show us the way.

It's Raining... Piss!

As a child, I always felt alone, even when there were many people around me. It's true I felt loved and listened to when I was at my nan's home but unfortunately it was not as often as I would have liked or needed. My little sister also offered comfort and companionship but, because she was younger, I couldn't share the pain of living that childhood. So, from a really young age, I always have been drawn to animals, any animals and all animals. Starting with my first furry friend, Twinkle, I would always and still do share my painful feelings with my four-legged friends. Animals are loyal and trustworthy, they listen, cuddle and do not judge or share your darkest secrets or, worse still, use any information against you.

As a vulnerable child, having someone or something to trust in was so important for my survival; it gave me hope, drive and determination. Most importantly, in my darkest moments when depression could have engulfed my young mind, it gave me the connection that I needed to see and feel a light that was worth pushing through to. Cuddling my cat showed me that there is love and goodness in the world, which is all that I ever wanted.

For me, I take a little too long to learn lessons. I have given too many chances and forgiven or forgotten unkind behaviour towards me as a child and as an adult, it seems, because I have always longed for a family, love and connections. For some that are no longer part of my life, it took adult maturity and motherhood to realise that there was no remorse on their part, so I said goodbye and do not regret leaving their poisonous ways behind me. One such person is my stepfather.

It was a long time after I stopped seeing him because of his callous behaviour towards my cat that I realised that I still carried great shame about a drunken action of his towards me.

On one occasion, when my mother and him must have been on friendly terms, but not so friendly that they were sleeping together, after a drunken night out together, she allowed him to sleep in my sister's bed, while my little sister snuggled in with her.

I wish that his giant bear-like snoring was the only inconsiderate behaviour that I had to encounter that night, but it wasn't. After hours of trying to get to sleep after he barged into the room, making himself comfortable, I finally fell back to sleep, only to be awoken by warm water pouring onto my face. I had no idea what it was, so I jumped up and screamed. To which my stepfather grunted and returned to bed.

Yes, he had just pissed on me. I felt both physically and mentally sick and I never mentioned it to anyone because like all the other experiences in my younger years I felt ashamed and to blame. Can you imagine that? It's ridiculous!

Years later, before I had decided to sever his vileness from my life, he laughed and joked about that night and I didn't have the strength at that time to speak up and tell him that his behaviour was out of order. I just took it because I still felt shame and I didn't want bad feelings about the experience resurfacing in front of others. I've now shed that shame and feeling of guilt about an incident for which the perpetrator felt no remorse about the effect that one of his many drunken actions had upon a little girl.

The behaviour of adults has a profound effect on the self-esteem of the young who are around them, whether intended or not. Be it good behaviour or not. For me, those around me as a child, their inappropriate manners and life, had both positive and negative effects on my whole being. I realised and clung to the knowledge that I didn't want to follow that path throughout my life's journey, with all of its twists and turns. I knew that I didn't want to be back in any of those childhood scenes.

However, with me I carried a bag of shame, shame for the life that I was forced to take part in, for mistakes made as a child, for having a mother who couldn't conquer her own demons. I lived with her demons as well, they became part of me and the low self-worth that was instilled in me through all the words that were spoken to me while I was still so impressionable.

Luckily within that childhood I had learnt to be resourceful, resilient and empathetic to others, at least. So I have bounced back from any setbacks, upsets or pain and I have gained and kept some incredible friends along the way, who helped me see that light that shines within me, that they have always seen.

It's true, having a support network to hug you, encourage you and to help you come through the dark days is so important, whether you are five years old or fifty years old and whatever situation that you find yourself in. It's through the support of fantastic friends that I have come through my most bleak moments and had the courage to allow others to read these words.

I Was the Bearer of Bad News

The sound of laughter and love drifted past us, piercing my heart deeper with each minute that passed and with each tear that my little sister shed. I felt helpless, useless, dark and generally wishing for the floor to swallow up my stupid pointless being. As her big sister and protector, I could do nothing to ease her distress or stop what had occurred earlier that day. I always thought it was my fault, for not trying harder, being better, being more. I was always to blame. We sat there on the cold, hard curb outside her school at the end of the school day, when most children were filling the air with screams of laughter, not sobs of pure pain. This was happening and this hurt was only going to increase with each day.

My little sister adored our mum. She was her little shadow, she yearned for her love and affection as any child does. She had not yet realised that the life we lived was not the same as each child that was now passing us, happily skipping off with their mothers to have a nutritious dinner that had been lovingly prepared and to play with their toys, in a safe and caring home.

Instead, I was telling my tiny, sensitive sister, who was still so small, that our mum was not coming home today and we wouldn't see her for a while because she had been taken to prison that morning and once again we were all alone. Okay, there were people stepping in, but we were alone, not with the one person in the world that should be there to protect us. That feeling hung around for years; the one person who should always be there for us wasn't then or on many other occasions.

Can you imagine what damage that causes to a child?

My sweet sister cuddled into me as if we were at home, not sitting in the gutter. She held me with the fear of a small child when losing those they love and need. We knew what came next. She would be palmed off to some kind person while our mum paid the price for whatever crime was committed this time. This wasn't the first time and certainly wouldn't be the last, we knew that. She had 'been on holiday' a few times at least – that's what we called a stint inside. Somehow that made it nicer, easier to bear, well for my mother anyway, and to be fair, it probably was a holiday for her. She could hide from many of her demons and the people who made them worse.

It wasn't a holiday for us, though. As much as life at home was difficult, it's where we always came back to and felt safe together. Certainly for us two innocent, impressionable girls, it was another embarrassment, another blow and more proof, proof that WE were not a 'normal', nice family. Okay, when my sister went to stay at different homes, the change was nice, beneficial and the normality was much needed for a little girl just wanting to be a child, loved and protected. Each child in this world deserves that.

Don't you agree?

It's strange that not one adult stopped to ask if we needed help or what was wrong. It was one of those times when you feel truly invisible; I'm sure you have experienced that.

Two girls crying and holding each other, sitting on the floor, while other 'human beings' carried on, as if we were not there, making our feelings of worthlessness even more ingrained into our little souls. Not one person showed any kindness, concern or acknowledgement. However, I now thank you fellow mums (as I'm now a mum to two fabulous girls). It taught me to always show concern for others in need and never walk on by, expecting someone else to step in!

My mum was well known on our estate, so probably the thought of those passing adults was, "Oh, another drama! We'd best stay away from that!"

Even though we lived on a council estate and it was full of normal working-class folk as well as those that didn't mind a bit of law breaking, we were certainly looked down upon, for several reasons. It cut me to the core that I felt beneath those around me and this was something that stayed with me for years. I had to work hard to remove that thought from my head and heart. 'The council estate kid, with a drunk criminal for a mother'. I gave myself that title and I held it close to my heart until one day I thought: "F!@# this! This is not who I am!"

We sat there outside Oxford Road School until the last of the happy families had disappeared back to their perfect homes.

"Where am I going?" she asked in her quiet voice. She was such a loving, generous child who just loved everyone. All I wanted to do was protect her and look after her, but I couldn't. That guilt stayed with me for many years. That I, as the elder child, couldn't protect her and give this little innocent a better life.

My sister went to stay with one of mum's friends this time. She would do the rounds over the years: friends, her family in Norfolk, her father and in her older years she spent time with a foster family. I know that I didn't see a great deal of her, not as much as I would have liked. I felt extreme guilt for years for not being able to care for her myself, after being told that I was too young. Which is ironic, as I had been caring for her for most of her little life.

For me, the maddest thing happened. I got to stay in our flat, on my own. I think I was about fifteen, maybe.

My father and stepmother didn't want me living with them and I wouldn't have gone there in a million years. The last time had been so awful, so I certainly didn't want to return, thank you very much. I felt unworthy and a lowlife anyway, I didn't need those who were meant to care for me to make this feeling more ingrained in my young mind.

So, as it was a relatively short sentence this time, I think about three months, I was to be able to stay where I was, so my mum had somewhere to return to when she came out and we still had a family home. My father and his wife were to keep an eye on me, make sure I was safe, fed and behaving myself. I still can't understand how this was allowed or if anyone ever knew about it. Maybe the powers-that-be had no idea, who knows?

Well, guess what? They didn't check on me, not really. Out of sight, out of mind! "Everything fine?" is all I got in passing. When I saw them on a Friday evening, which was the night that my grandparents visited them, so it made visiting my father's home a little more tolerable, I went to collect my child maintenance from my dad, which was – wait for it – £5! He had been giving me the money for a little while as it saved my mum from drinking it away. I think she could only get two bottles of sherry with that even back in the eighties. I, of course, spent it on food or probably sweeties.

So, I stayed in our flat on my own for the duration of my mother being on her holidays. I thought it was so cool, at first. I really wasn't a party girl; I had a couple of great friends who stayed over. Boys tended to stay away from me – I thought it was because I was ugly and weird but I think it may have had more to do with the talks that my mum would give any boy that came near me. She would scare the absolute shit out of them and normally she would be totally pissed so the whole experience would be a hundred times worse for the poor victim. She would forget about this little scene and the next time she encountered the poor boy, she would either be super nice or start all over again, so hence no chance of a teenage pregnancy for me. Thanks, Mum, and I really mean that!

So even though I thought I was some kind of cosmopolitan kid, living in my own apartment, truth be told I was lonely, afraid, sad and extremely angry with everyone around me. I felt abandoned, unwanted and unlovable, once again. Would I ever be wanted? This constantly went through my mind. I actually didn't want to be strong all the time, I wanted someone to care for me, not to just think or say, "Sophie will be okay, she's strong."

It's lucky that by this point I had already learnt so many unconventional ways to live, eat and survive. All methods that I certainly would not encourage in my own beautiful daughters and have not had to participate in for over thirty years, thankfully. However, I am thankful that as a child who only had myself to depend on, I had these skills.

For a while, my life was a little bittersweet whilst she was away. The flat wasn't full of the kind of people most mothers want their kids to stay away from. There was respite from that, as well as shoplifting, drink, drugs and the cruel words that used to flow from her mouth when she was drunk. I started to live and find out who I was and what I wanted in life. This may have been the first time the thought that I didn't need to be like 'her' entered my mind. That I didn't need to end up like these people who so regularly visited our home but never brought any love or happiness. All they seemed to bring were black clouds, negativity and more pain.

However, I missed my mum, in a way. I was still a child, even though she hadn't been a mum for years, really. She was still my mother and should have been my protector and I was holding onto those last moments because I knew times and myself were changing; this madness wouldn't always surround me.

I missed my little friend, my sister, tremendously. I had always adored her, so being away from her was extremely hard for me to bear. I cried a lot. I wanted her life to be so different from mine, growing up. I wanted her to have a childhood. I didn't want her to encounter the people or activities that I had as I grew into a young woman. I wanted her to have a chance, love, safety and security. That's probably why I supported my stepfather's application for custody of her, which in hindsight, in my opinion, was a dire mistake all round. This was another childhood mistake for which I carried a lot of guilt around for years, but I was a child and a child without the guidance that I needed.

Even though the flat was full to the brim with things, with other people's things, with other people's history, it always felt empty, like an empty box, and I was just rolling around in it, waiting. I feared the nights, I feared noises, I feared people and I was petrified as to what could happen if people found out I was there alone. I was literally totally alone.

The other side of the coin was I was able to get my own food. I still had no idea about cooking a proper meal, but I tried. My good friend from school came to stay some days and that was a great experience for me to share my space with someone as warm and crazy as she was. She helped me start to learn that 'normal' isn't always so great and I mean that in the nicest way. I started to feel I could express myself, be it verbally, the way I dressed or what I ate. My mother always had a comment to enlighten me as to what I was doing wrong, so it was great not to experience that for a while. Constant criticism and doubt are self-esteem killers and stop any type of positive progress or growth.

It was during this prison spell I went to visit my mum as she was in a local prison, which she had 'visited' many times before. East Sutton Park is still there today and it is set in the most beautiful surroundings. I remember that one of my mum's best friends Ross took me to see her. I can't recall if we drove or took the bus. Knowing Ross, we probably went by taxi as he was no doubt pissed. Ross was a very flamboyant character and my mother adored him and he her. By this point in my life, as I developed into a young woman, he normally treated me with disdain and liked to make me feel uncomfortable, which my mum found hysterical.

The thing that I remember most about the prison are the huge dark wood doors, they were so imposing for a nervous teenager. Those colossal oak doors are etched on my mind and what was just a physical barrier to my mum back then now appear in my mind often when I think about how distant she always was to me; there was always a barrier, something she was locked behind.

However, it was like a stately home, rather than somewhere to keep wrongdoers. It really seemed like a holiday camp, the prisoners wandering around the grounds, laughing and chatting, enjoying the splendour of this gorgeous manor house.

My mum seemed sober but really who could tell. She had always been very slim, I think it was from being malnourished as a child and then as an adult with the choice between food or alcohol, booze always won, hands down. Being in there she had gained some weight; she put it down to the doughnuts that they made. I had never seen her eat a doughnut in my life, so I thought they must be temptingly good! She made several 'special friends' during her little spells in the holiday camps, which began when she was about nineteen years old or maybe slightly younger. I guess by this point it felt like a home from home.

I felt sad for my mum for being in prison, even though she actually looked quite well and the building looked absolutely wonderful, like something out of a period drama rather than *The Bill*. On the other hand, I felt deep rage and bitterness: why couldn't she get her life sorted out, why didn't she love us enough to stop with her addictions and all this crime and why were we always punished by her behaviour?

I often wondered, "Why are our lives like this?" I never received an answer.

Ultimately, I just wanted her to be my mum, that's all I have ever wanted. Even now I long to have a mum to help when times are tough and just to be held and loved by a woman who loves me for who I am.

Ross and my mum were as animated as ever, laughing, chatting and cracking jokes, normally at other people's expense and I wasn't immune from their unkindness, either. It is only as I grew into an adult that I started to understand why those around me would ridicule me as a teenager, as I started to develop and mature. I use the word mature rather loosely, as I didn't really mature, and I certainly wasn't very womanly. However, I was an easy target to those that wanted a little spiteful joke. My lack of growth was probably because of my irregular and strange eating patterns as a kid. It's only as I have reflected seriously on those times that I realise certain elements of that time in my life have had such an impact on my whole bloody life! Don't get me wrong, not always in a bad way. Believe me 'Every cloud does have a silver lining'. If you look a little bit deeper!

I spent the brief time opposite my mum looking around me in nervous awe. All these women were like my mother, they were all separated from their children, who were sitting across from them. It was one of the first moments that I realised I wasn't the only child that had a dysfunctional childhood. There were many tears shed in that room, the emotion was sorrowfully tangible.

As we left, I saw deep sadness in my mum's eyes; I didn't know if it was sorrow because I was leaving and she loved me. Was she sorry? Or was it because she couldn't take much more of prison? For all the elements that were surprisingly pleasant, it could also be brutal. I heard her speak with her friends when she came home about drink, drugs, violence and abuse. She tried hard in prison to stay much more sober as she wanted to stay in control of herself in situations that could be potentially extremely dangerous. This hurt me for some time because I wondered why she couldn't do the same on the outside, for the sake of her children. At the time, and for some time after, it was another reinforcement that she didn't love me. I now know that the situation was a lot more complex than that.

As the heavy wooden doors slowly shut behind us, I pushed back the tears that were swelling up inside of my fragile form; by fragile I mean that I was at breaking point. I was a teenager dealing with hormones, self-doubt and loathing, the loss of my mum and sister. The turmoil of my short life had taken its toll on me. I was lost, broken and alone as a young teen.

By this point in my life, I had learnt that crying solved nothing by any means, it just made you vulnerable to those that would use you. I definitely wouldn't receive any sympathetic words from Ross, don't even mention the word hug! He would fall about laughing if I said I needed comfort. Then he would proceed to tell me to stop making a scene and pull my socks up.

This time in my young life certainly had an impact on me for a long time after, as did many other experiences. That feeling of loneliness never really left. It was the beginning of the end of my childhood and it was the end of the relationship with my mum. Even though we had never had the conventional mother-daughter relationship by any stretch of the imagination, the loss and hurt continued. It was that day that I knew I had to escape as soon as I could. I had to get out of that environment and stay out or fast-forward twenty years and maybe it would be my daughter visiting me... and so the cycle would continue!

Always one to go against the grain, I thought, "F@#* that, I'm not ending up here!"

And I broke that shitty, life-sapping, soul-destroying evil cycle!

Never Judge A Book By It's Cover

My mum was an extremely intelligent, cultured, creative, beautiful woman, with so much to give her family and the wider world. It is so unfortunate that she succumbed to the evil clutches of alcohol. On the rare occasion that her genius shone through, I lapped it up, knowing that it may be some time before the next moment of joy came from her.

One of these sweet moments, which was so simple and innocent, was when my mum and I used to act out *Oliver Twist* in our living room. I would be Oliver and she would be Mr Bumble and we would giggle and perform our hearts out as we delivered Oscar-winning performances, in my opinion, of the "Please Sir, can I have some more" scene. In my mind, as I enjoyed this time with her, I was actually wishing, "Please, Mum, can I have more of this?" Of course, normal behaviour always returned swiftly and quite often brutally.

I love to read and absorb information. Even as a young girl, I loved a good story, although my reading and spelling levels were extremely below average. Over time, as a young adult, with the help of persistence and a faithful dictionary, I improved both, enjoying losing myself in other people's stories and adventures.

This love certainly stems from my mum, as she would always be reading, quite often into the early hours. She had piles and piles of books stacked in her bedroom, covering all kinds of subjects, from the history of Britain to biographies, like the one she had on Brigitte Bardot, who she adored. At a fairly young age, this is where I saw for the first time a picture of a naked lady kissing another lady, which in the late seventies was quite shocking, particularly to a young impressionable girl.

My mum had so much knowledge and talent, I always looked at her and thought that I would never be able to compete with her beauty and intelligence. Being told that I was stupid and ugly no doubt added to me feeling that I was living in her shadow, and even when I left home I always felt like the plain Jane because those feelings had been deeply ingrained.

As I became a teenager, I got cross and upset at how much she had wasted her life with her choices. As I fought to understand my school lessons and achieve at least average grades at school, she threw away the chance to do and be whatever she desired by choosing to stay in her dark but safe comfort zone. As I have matured and experienced more, I realised more about her position and about the choices that she made. I am no longer cross, but I feel sorrow for what the world missed out on because this woman could have achieved incredible things.

Maybe she also knew this fact and that's why she tried sometimes, in her own oddball way, to make me more.

We had a little black and white telly perched on an antique table in our living room. While all my friends would rush home after school to watch the children's programmes that were beginning to become more popular, my mum very rarely allowed me to watch them.

"That tosh will rot your brain," she would snipe at me. Now there is definitely some truth in that, but I often wondered if she was just being mean. Nowadays, as a mum myself, I'm glad that I didn't just get plonked in front of the telly as a child because I now encourage my kids to do more than stare at a screen, although quite a lot of the time I have very little success there.

Reflecting on my mother's wasted talents and lost dreams now, it makes me more determined to live to my own full potential. Not only that, I will endeavour to encourage anyone that will listen to chase their dreams passionately and never give up. *Never give up, never ever!*

Not Turkish Delight

A period of dark turmoil for me was when my mother and a friend of hers, who happened to be a local 'lady of the night', befriended a couple of Turkish brothers, who had just arrived in England.

Back in the eighties, immigrants were fairly rare where I lived. My mother, always being attracted to exotic and flamboyant characters, was drawn to their swanky, sophisticated ways and dress. It was a welcome break for her from the usual 'geezer' that frequented the pubs that she enjoyed being in.

I personally couldn't stand either of the men. They were out for themselves and they had no thought for anyone else. As a teen, I found them totally slimy and predatory.

By choice I would never be alone with them or leave my sister with them.

Unfortunately, it seemed that my mum, who was just longing to be loved, truly loved and fell head over heels in love with one of the brothers. I don't remember which and it really doesn't matter because it didn't last. As soon as it became clear that she wouldn't marry him, he moved onto another woman who he had waiting in the wings who would!

During the time that he was in our home, she was consumed in making sure that he was happy and cared for. Some normality even arose, with my mum cooking regularly and the appearance of a happy family emerging. Well, she was happy – at least hoping to be.

One time that I dared to mention that he had a huge dinner plate full of food and us girls didn't, she whacked me in the face and gave me a nosebleed.

I was ecstatic when these two slime bags disappeared off the scene. I guess for my mum, it was just another abandonment after taking her love.

Once again, she was left alone!

Was It Work?

As local pubs in my hometown began to close, one of them being the pub that was just a few doors down from my childhood home, I giggled that they were closing after losing my mother's business after her death. That was probably very poor taste on my part.

The pub that was just a stone's throw from our front door was my mother's second home. She loved the atmosphere of the pub culture, different characters coming together, laughing, connecting and without doubt the drama that went along with people trying to escape their lives with the use of alcohol.

She worked there for a while, on and off. This job suited her to a tee as she was such a social creature. Being surrounded by people, noise and drama helped her not think about things that hurt her heart and of course all the free drinks were whole-heartedly accepted.

I often thought about how my mother settled for so much less than she deserved, as far as men, personal choices and jobs were concerned. She was a barmaid in several pubs in the local town and she picked fruit in the summer months. She had many more jobs, some of them sounding quite fabulous before she succumbed to drink and I came along.

Some of my fondest memories of childhood are the ones that I spent running around a raspberry field, climbing trees and enjoying the freedom of being a child. I loved it when my mum had a job, it made everything easier and brighter.

My mum seemed a lot happier as well; she had the connection of the other ladies and she was providing for herself and her girls, not relying on anyone else.

The smell and taste of raspberries always brings a smile to my lips, even now. Those bright days spent in the sunshine being a child were just the best and the memory of them still brings me great joy.

We needed more days like that. We may have survived as a family unit if we had – or that's what I like to think anyway.

Fun Days, Crazy Days...
Oh Crazy Days Were Every Day!

My mother had a collection of eccentric friends, from the most favourite gay friend, Ross, to James, the fantastically gorgeous hairdresser, who she gave her heart to. Not forgetting the infamous Tim, who had lovely long blond hair and a beard and was always, I mean always smiling. Apparently 'back in the day' he was known to ride his motorbike around our area completely naked! My mum had a soft spot for his laid-back hippie nature.

Our home was normally filled with an array of people from all walks of life, telling their fabulously embellished stories full of excitement and intrigue around a glass or ten of something. There were a lot of criminals of all levels and degrees but also many folk that you would not expect to find in the council house of a local criminal. So as long as it was not the middle of the night when they decided to descend on our little flat, which often it was and I was always awoken to be introduced, I was happy to meet them and I often listened with intrigue to their lives and those that they were freely talking about.

I learnt at a young age how to communicate with all sorts of people and put on a show, if needs be. Another skill or curse that I acquired growing up was the ability to read people and situations extremely well, so I would act in the correct manner as to not cause any trouble, not be noticed or even take the limelight off someone else. This has been a blessing and a curse throughout my life because it has always meant that I have monitored my behaviour and acted accordingly to those around me. This is not always a good thing and has definitely stopped me stepping into the light and shining... *Thank heavens, I'm past that phase!*

Realising that I am not responsible for another's attitude or actions has been truly liberating. For those of you that are still in a traumatic environment or once was, the moment that you take responsibility for your feelings and emotions only, you will start to live your full life.

I can't remember too many successful or truly pleasant outings with my mum – outings that a child would enjoy, that is. One memory I do relish is a trip to a local restaurant called Dixies; it was a thrilling and delicious time. It was an American diner that served the most mouth-watering burgers that I yearned for. There was an array of yummy delights and I filled my little tummy, making it look like a balloon just about to pop.

Even though a visit there didn't happen often, probably less than a handful of times, I can still smell the aroma and feel the feelings of anticipation I had as a teen after being informed we were going there. Unfortunately, Dixies shut many years ago, otherwise I think that I would still visit there now to reflect on those deliciously, dare I say it, family times.

When my mum was not so flash, or just skint, it was a trip to Pizza Hut, where we would fill our tummies on a selection of delights and then just get up and leave. This occurred many times in my childhood years and, for a long time, I didn't realise that my mum was leaving without paying. As I became more aware, it was so shameful to me.

As I look back on it, I realise, as wrong as it was, I probably wouldn't have eaten otherwise. I often think of those times when I take my own daughters to Pizza Hut and wonder what they would do if I got up and left without paying. They'd probably think that I had at last lost my very last marble. No, hang on, that left years ago!

Special celebrations are still quite daunting for me these days. Even though I adore my own children and love seeing their beaming faces when receiving gifts, Christmas and birthdays always plunge me backwards in time. Luckily, I spent some time with my grandparents over any celebration period. They would spoil me and feed me up. My nanny would always make a birthday cake, just for me. I felt loved and like I was worthy of a celebration. However, at home, the feel and flow of Christmas depended on whether my mum had had some 'successful shopping trips' and how drunk people got. Would there be a fight, would the police visit or maybe something even more festive mood dampening?

Birthdays! Well, for children, they were not really celebrated... I mean, really, how do you celebrate a kid's birthday back in the seventies or eighties? An adult, that's a different matter... that's easy, get drunk.

I did have one birthday party when I think I was about seven or maybe eight, and it turned into a disaster. For me, anyway.

A bunch of girls running around screaming, eating jelly and ice cream and generally being silly; bliss! I was in my element and for once it was all about me, with no dramas...until my stepdad decided to play the authoritarian father. We had all played many party games quite happily; pass the parcel, musical bumps and musical statues had all passed by without any hiccups. Then we moved onto finding ten pence pieces that had been hidden in that bloody cabbage patch that was growing in our garden – that darned cabbage patch!

As we all ran around finding our hidden treasure, I was just thinking about how many sweeties that I could buy at the shop with my loot. My stepfather had only hidden about £2 in 10p coins, but it was enough for our small collection of girls to get excited about as we rushed around the cabbages, rummaging through them and discovering a small army of slugs on the way. We giggled and skipped around enjoying the July sun. I felt so happy to be in the centre of this childish fun and for the happiness in our home. It seemed like heaven!

Unfortunately, this childhood bliss didn't last that long and I came crashing back to earth with a hell-fire bump. One of my little friends did not find any shining little coins, so as the rest of us young girls giggled and screamed with delight she bawled her eyes out and stamped her feet. My stepfather, who was always so accommodating and understanding to anyone outside of our family, turned to me.

"Soph, give her your money," he ordered roughly, knowing he could be as mean as he liked to me.

I stood there with the hot sun beating down on my back in my party dress holding my little stash of money in my sweating palm, yet again disappointed but truly not surprised that I was being made to give up something of mine.

As a group, we all said we would give the crying child 10p each quite happily, but my stepfather towered over me and ordered me to hand over my whole stash. I was always totally petrified of him, especially when he let his brutish side surface. However, even back then, being threatened or forced to do something made my hackles raise, like a cat, and I hissed, "No!" while pressing my feet into the ground with my hands on my hips. "She should have looked harder and found her own. We will all give her one coin," I offered generously.

At the threat to his manhood in front of an audience, albeit a gaggle of little girls, he leant over me and grabbed my hand, prising my pennies out of my hand, while I tried hard to hang onto them, gritting my teeth and giving him a steely look. Of course, he won and he smirked at me, passing my find to the screaming child. I was hurt, angry and shamed in front of my friends, at *my birthday party!*

"Now, you can spend the rest of the day in bed, for being disobedient." He laughed as he pointed to the back door.

I stood there in total surprise. Seriously, this felt just so cruel…spending my birthday in bed while my party guests enjoyed themselves… he must be joking!

"Go on, get to bed before I decide to smack you," he screamed.

I trudged indoors, refusing to cry or allow him to have any more power over me as the other little girls looked on in shock.

I lay in my bunk bed for the rest of the afternoon listening to giggling and happiness as I thought about when I could live a life where no one but me could control me. I yearned for that day and I knew it would surely come just as the sun would rise the next day.

As the adults got merrier and started to enjoy themselves more, forgetting about the children, my friends came into my room and crowded around my bed. They all seemed concerned and sad that I was exiled from my own celebration but I had already learnt to rise above the present moment. He would not control my emotions, I would not allow him.

This group of girls chatted to me and we laughed as we spoke about all the things that were important to girls of that age, Polly Pocket, strawberry shortcake and *have you seen the new Cindy doll*? That we all yearned for!

After the girls left, I refused to get up as I wouldn't give him the satisfaction of telling me to go back to bed or gloat that I missed my own birthday party. My mother was surprisingly quiet during the afternoon celebrations. I don't know if it was because she was frightened of his anger or because she enjoyed my shame and sorrow. I look back and find it quite funny that I spent my birthday in bed, with my friends coming to court like I was a regal queen.

As I travelled through my stormy childhood, no one, not anyone could control how I felt! Or what I thought! They may do something that was cruel or horrendous, but I controlled whether or not I got up, dusted myself off and walked away sticking up two fingers as I did.

School: The Place To Be

For me as a child, school was my safe haven. I loved it: the community, the innocence and the ability to escape everything that troubled me at home, even though, from a very young age, I always felt like the poor snotty kid of the class. I felt beneath and intimidated by the teachers and the other children alike. I allowed myself to carry this into adulthood, which laid me bare to be treated wrongly because I always felt less… I believed that I was ugly, fat, unintelligent and generally a complete waste of space.

I'm not sure if anyone in my school knew about my home life or how I felt. No one ever broached the subject with me or offered me help. It was obvious that I struggled at school with a lot of the basic stuff and I just muddled through. As I got older, I just bluffed my way through situations, exams, jobs and life in general.

I was very creative, whether it was putting on a show in primary school, which involved singing and dancing with a friend, or building sets for our Oscar-winning performances to elaborate stories that I wrote in secondary school, which were no doubt troublesome to read because of the terrible spelling. However, I always felt stupid, untalented and just behind everyone. This feeling didn't really ever leave and, yes, it's still lurking in the back of my mind and heart. The only difference now is that I think to myself, "What's the worst that could happen? Because it's already happened to me, several times. And do you know what? I got up from that."

Any hating, mistakes or failures have never stopped me and never will because my CHOICE is now to thrive not just survive!

It seems that school was just a place of refuge for me. I wasn't really encouraged, inspired or believed in, so I didn't follow any great thought out path, like most of my school peers.

I really wanted to go to college and continue to study, I wanted to find a dream and follow it, but unfortunately I needed to leave school and earn money as I didn't have the luxury of parents supporting and encouraging me to better myself. So, I went off and found myself a job, the only job that I could without the best grades. I got a retail YTS (Youth Training Scheme) job paying just £28.00 per week.

Now, this job was fabulously fun. Okay, it wasn't really what I wanted to do initially, however I learnt so much and I met the most splendid people, it really set me up for my future career. I worked in a fancy dress shop, which also sold theatrical make up and props; it really was the best 'first job' that I could have had.

It was a continuation of flamboyant folk telling their interesting stories, full of adult adventures and lives that seemed a world away from mine at home. I started to grow up and distance myself from life at my mum's flat, even though for a time I still lived there.

It doesn't matter where we start out in life, what matters is knowing that you are not going to stay there, that your end destination can and will be a million miles away!

It seems to me now as I sit here, after unleashing the beast from its bag and I watch it disappear into thin air, with no power or grip upon me anymore, I feel sorrow for it and all those that were held by its force.

I realise that even though I escaped the physical bohemian place of my childhood, all those years ago when

I left, I hadn't really escaped its grip, but in fact I had hidden the truth of it under this cloak of pretend *bohemia.*

Once I let go of the fabricated version, I truly escaped. I left the shame and guilt behind and my true worth started coming into view... I like the view!

I give thanks to the views and ideas that I once held because they protected me for a time. They served their purpose and helped me enter a better world. But I should have kissed them goodbye years ago before I started to rely on them and use them as a reason for not becoming *ME* or at least trying to fulfil my true individual potential.

So here I sit, a whole lot lighter than when I began this writing journey, no longer afraid that people will guess who I really am, where I come from or even their views about it.

I'm grateful for the creative journey that this endeavour has taken me on and through. I feel blessed that I've been able to shed the skin that I once hid beneath and become who I really am, who I feel comfortable with... so here I am, completely bare and exposed!

I'm relieved... thank you.

Time To Shine

True growth and strength comes from the trails that we encounter throughout our life's journey and I am truly grateful for what I've always called my bohemian childhood. It helped mould me into the woman that I am, and I am now proud of who I was and who I am.

It is a true saying "That which doesn't kill us, makes us stronger" and we must be thankful for the ability to grow, to overcome and shine. Without it, we would remain stagnant, we would not fulfil our potential and there would be no point to us or life.

Maybe it's hard whilst going through trials and dramas to see or, indeed, feel the reasoning behind it, or even some days have the strength to push through the shit. It's on those days that we first must rest, give ourselves a break, love and understand ourselves and then we must, for we have no other choice, get up, dust ourselves off and kick that darkness firmly into the past.

If I, as a child – and children who have endured far worse than me – can come through darkness and shine lights on the world with joy and love, then as adults we can squash all the crap that comes our way because we are more powerful than we give ourselves credit for.

With that power we must fulfil our potential and live the beautiful life that we hold in our mind's eye, enjoying our time here on earth.

I realised throughout this journey of stepping back into the past, of reminiscing and writing, that I actually am a lot stronger and courageous than I ever gave myself credit for. My being, light, soul or my personality, whatever you wish to call it, is amazingly powerful, it's what drives me. I've come to know that it is my soul that pushed me to power through and not give up, when I could have quite easily laid down and slept forever.

I'm thankful for the stubborn lioness that lies deep inside me, purring with satisfaction most of the time, but when needed roars ferociously. I know that it is not just me that has this power, this ability to overcome, to stick two fingers up at the pain that once haunted me. We all can and must come to know our inner strength and allow it to guide and push us on.

Mum and Dad, I Love You

And to my mum and dad, the people who made me and should have protected me, helped me grow and fulfil my potential, I say, "I wish someone had helped you with the pain that you carried around, because then you may have lived the lives that you wanted and found happiness. May you now both *'Rest in peace'*."

Gratitude

Thank you for taking the time to read my diary entries. I decided to not make this into a story and share it with you instead, just as I wrote it, remembering one episode at a time, stepping back in time and watching my own life play out. One drama seemed to lead to another, unlocking something that had been buried within me for years. Of course, I could have delved deeper, rediscovered even more and shared much more, but maybe now is not the time. Perhaps one day you will be reading or seeing the whole story. I have shared exactly what resurfaced, exactly as it did, and I'm thankful for the opportunity and encouragement to do so.

I hope by sharing my journey it will help others to shed the shame of their past and not take so long to realise their own potential!

Printed in Great Britain
by Amazon